Empyrean *Winter 2025*

A QUARTERLY OF ARTS AND LITERATURE
PUBLISHED INDEPENDENTLY

Editor-in-Chief

Kaylyn Dunn

Sponsored by

Kada's Bookstore

Special Additions by

Katherine Edgren
Arnold Johnston
Jessica Knuth

https://www.empyreanliterarymagazine.com/

Contents

ISSUE 16: VOL. 4, NO. 4

Introduction

IN A world often obsessed with renewal, youth, and progress, we delve into one of the most profound and paradoxical themes: decay. We invite you to pause and reflect on the quiet dignity, haunting beauty, and inevitable truth embedded in decay. Through the voices of thirty-four gifted contributors, we explore how decay manifests in our lives.

Decay is not merely the end; it is also a beginning. It is the slow unraveling that reveals hidden layers, the erosion that uncovers truths buried beneath surface appearances. In literature, decay has long been a muse, an allegory for mortality, change, and the fleeting nature of existence. Our contributors capture this nuance, offering stories, poems, essays, and reflections that challenge us to see broken strength in the crumbling, and meaning in the fading.

We hope this collection sparks a recognition of the bittersweet, often contradictory truths embedded in decay: that in every end, there is a beginning; that the inevitable decline is intertwined with the potential for renewal. As you journey through these pages, may you find in the shadows of decay a space for a deeper appreciation for the fleeting, precious nature of life itself.

We are grateful to each of our thirty-one contributors for their courage to explore this theme with honesty and artistry.

Daddy

1st Place Nonfiction Winner   Jessica Knuth

The moon is only a white disc, pulsing, like the edge of a thumbnail imprinted in the sky. Daddy's wind chimes move with the breeze, as if to whisper how far away he has suddenly become. Somewhere in another time and place, I feel as though I will see him again, and all this time that has passed will mean nothing. It will be like he was just sleeping, like I was.

He died February 17th. His tombstone would later read the 18th, since it was after midnight when the coroner arrived at our house to pronounce him dead, but he died the 17th. It wasn't a surprise to anyone but me, though I thought I had prepared myself for it. He fell ill in late September. It was a metastatic tumor that originated years ago in his colon but had now attached itself to his brain. By October, it had destroyed his ability to walk. He was confined to a hospital bed that we set up in his and my mother's bedroom. He wanted to die at home. By November, half of his memories were gone. He spoke of things no one understood, of people he had never actually known. He began to hallucinate, to lie on his back and grab at the air with his hands, as if something was floating there and he was trying to catch it. He spoke of a man named Charlie with big legs, said he saw him outside the window walking through the field, or sitting in the rocking chair beside his bed. But no one else did.

By December, we were told he could die at any time. The doctors could do nothing else for him. The tumor was inoperable and it had long stopped responding to chemotherapy and radiation. The cancer swam from cerebellum to cortex, eating and eating like a shark. I was a freshman in college and living in a dorm at the university I attended on the opposite side of the state. I kept telling myself that he wouldn't die. It wasn't even a possibility. Cancer was nothing new to my father. In the past seven years, he had undergone countless surgeries and rounds of chemotherapy and radiation to combat tumors in his colon, his pancreas, his neck. It had even showed up in his brain exactly one year prior, though that time the surgeon was able to remove it. Each time the cancer resurfaced, we experienced months of sadness and worry. But each time he got better and there was hope again. I kept telling myself that this was no different, that the cancer would go away this time like it had gone away in the past.

When I came home for Christmas break, I saw how bad things really were. I spent the month home from school helping my mom take care of him. I saw how much work Dad was, how she had to lift him in bed and bathe him, shampoo his hair, put him on the bedpan, change his diapers. He had never been this sick or unresponsive. Sometimes he didn't recognize me. My mother took a leave of absence from her job to become his full-time nurse. He had become bedridden in early October and he died in February. My mother did not leave the house once until after his funeral. Not to buy groceries. Not to pick up the mail. Not to go shopping. Not even to go for a walk. I don't know if

she was scared to leave him or if she felt guilty. If
he couldn't leave, she wouldn't either. Our family
helped as much as they could. My brother ran my
mother's errands. My father's sisters brought
covered dishes of food so Mom wouldn't have to
cook. When I was home, I did the grocery
shopping. I picked up mail from the post office. I
bought her cigarettes, even though I hated her
smoking. By then, I felt like that's all she had left.
She sat in the kitchen staring off into nothing,
sucking and sucking the cigarettes until everything
she felt burned out into a pile of ash.

Mom didn't want to put up a Christmas tree that
year, so I did it for her. It was small and sparse with
gaping bald spots between the branches.
Traditionally for Christmas, she and I would spend
days decorating. We would drape garland around
the front porch columns and along the mantle. We
would tape Christmas cards sent from our friends
and family around the doorframe that separated the
kitchen from the living room. There would be fake
snow on the coffee table and candles shaped like
little fat snowmen and Santa and his elves. There
were other candles on top of the piano, tall skinny
ones that were red and green and gold. The tree
always had the same ornaments, and we hung them
together onto the branches while we sang Christmas
songs and baked sugar cookies that tasted horrible,
but we ate them anyway. Every year it was
comforting to pull out that box of ornaments and
resurrect forgotten memories. There was the paper
apple my brother made when he was a child, the
little fat mouse wearing a Santa hat given to me by
my old babysitter, the crystal snowflake that
changed colors when it caught the light. But my

favorite was a little blue stocking. I had made it out of clay in my third-grade art class and couldn't wait for my parents to see it. When Dad picked me up from school that day, I unzipped my backpack to show him, but it fell onto the ground, and the tip of the stocking broke off. I stood there crying and wiping my eyes on my sweater as he gathered up the pieces. He glued them back together when we got home. It didn't look as nice as it originally had, but it held together, and it holds still. That's the only ornament I put on our tree the year he was dying.

Daddy couldn't get out of bed to open presents on Christmas morning. When I was a little girl I would wake first, run out of my room to see the presents scattered all around, and then rally everyone else to come gather around the tree. Dad was always the last to stir, taking time to make his coffee, but we never started without him. This year we didn't have a choice. It was just my mother and I that morning, and she had been awake long before I was, watching infomercials on television about makeup that could reduce the appearance of fine lines and wrinkles.

"Merry Christmas," I said, sleep still in my eyes.

"Merry Christmas."

I didn't ask her if she was ready to open presents. For the first time in my life, I was actually dreading it, and I could tell she was too, but she stood up from her chair and sat down on the rug beside the Christmas tree. I sat across from her in my usual space. Dad's chair was empty. The room was awkward and quiet. The oxygen machine hissed and beeped through Daddy's open doorway at the end of the hall. I kept waiting to hear the wooden floorboards creaking and to see him walk into the room with a cup of coffee in his right hand. We didn't get out the video camera like we normally would have. We just opened our gifts in silence, thanking each other when appropriate. It was over very quickly. By the time we finished, neither of us could remember anything the other person had bought for them. We sat there for a moment among the discarded wrapping paper and empty cardboard boxes, our minds someplace else.

Later that day, after my brother had opened gifts with his wife and daughter, they came to our house. We took all of the gifts we had for Dad into his bedroom to show him. He couldn't open them on his own, so my mother did it for him. She made a fuss over each one. "Look at these new pajamas!" she said, holding them up in the air so he could see. It was the same way she pointed out presents to my niece at her first birthday party. After the second present, Dad didn't even look at her anymore. He just stared out the window, and everyone cried a little bit without acknowledging it. We were all thinking the same thing—that he would never be able to use any of the presents we had bought for him, but I kept praying that things would turn around. Maybe he would wake up in the morning and be able to walk again. Maybe he would smile or call out our names when we walked in the room. Maybe he could be Daddy again, and not the man lying in bed who sometimes knew us and sometimes did not.

Classes started up again at my university on January 14th. I drove back to school the day before

to settle into my dorm, leaving Mom at home alone
to care for Dad. My roommate had decided not to
return to school that semester, so I had the room all
to myself. I thought I would like the privacy. I had
plenty of space to store all my things. But once my
clothes were hung in the closet and there was
nothing else to do, the loneliness set in, along with
the regret. I lay in bed staring at the concrete walls
thinking of Daddy. It was hard sleeping that night
and even harder to wake up and get ready the next
morning. I only had two classes that day, but I
didn't pay attention in either of them. I went back to
the dorm and lay awake all night. I thought about
my mother taking care of Dad on her own again,
struggling to lift him, sitting in the kitchen smoking
cigarettes. But more than that, I thought about that
blank look in his eyes, the way he couldn't carry a
conversation, the way he couldn't speak at all. Early
that next morning, instead of going to class, I
packed everything I could fit into my car and sat
down on the front steps of my building. The sun
hadn't been up long, and the sky was gray and cold.
Nothing moved. It was as if I was the only person
awake in the world. I got into my car, started the
engine, and drove home for good without calling to
ask Mom if it was okay. It was the first grown-up
decision I ever had to make, but I didn't hesitate. I
enrolled in our hometown community college on
January 17th. Daddy died exactly one month later.

I hated taking classes at the community college
because most of the people I'd just graduated from
high school with the previous summer were
enrolled there. When I was at the university, I felt
like I was far away from home and doing something

admirable, making something of myself, surviving on my own. But sitting in class next to the same old faces and same old names, looking out the window at the same sad stretch of lonely highway I had lived along my entire life made me wonder if coming home was the right decision after all.

As I drove home from class snow was beginning to fall. Thin and light as powder, it dusted the tops of the mountains and limbs of the trees. My mother was sitting in the living room smoking a cigarette and watching soap operas. She asked me about class. I asked her about Daddy. Before she could answer, he groaned from the other room, calling out for her. She didn't move.

"He's been asking me to pray with him all day," she said.

"About what?" I asked, dropping my purse onto the couch and taking off my coat. She didn't answer for a moment, like the words were stuck in her throat. I realized she was trying not to cry.

"For it to be over."

She exhaled and wiped her eyes. I wanted to ask her what—for what to be over—and then I realized. I wanted Mom to stop talking. I wanted to run. Like that time when I was ten and I found my kitten dead in the garage, or the time I was fifteen and my first boyfriend broke my heart. I wanted to run away, and fall asleep someplace safe, and wake up again like nothing ever happened. Like it was all a really long and really horrible dream. But I heard Daddy calling her name again and I knew that running away would solve nothing. He was dying. He was ready to.

Even though he was asking for Mom, I went to Daddy's room to see what he needed. I walked down the hall and turned the corner. He was lying among the bed sheets, his hair matted and his eyes wild.

"Hi Daddy," I said, trying my best to appear calm. He looked like a scared animal, like the baby deer my aunt had rescued from the woods behind her house after its mother had been killed by a car. Those same wild eyes, haunting and afraid. Not my Daddy's eyes.

I sat down on the corner of the bed, taking his hand in mine. He was shaking.

"How are you feeling today?" I asked, not sure if he even knew I was his daughter.

He didn't answer, but his hand stopped shaking, so I just held onto it. He laid his head against the pillow. There was a glass of water on the nightstand beside his bed, and I held it against his lips for him to drink. He tilted his head back and I wiped the water from his chin. When he was finished, he reached his shaking hand out for me to hang onto. He was so helpless. I had the urge to run away again. If I ran away none of this would be real. I watched his shaking fingers dance in the air, and I grabbed onto him, remembering all the times he held my hand when I needed it. When he taught me to walk, to hold a fishing pole, to ride my bike. He had always been there for me when no one else had. He was always the one to comfort me when something had gone wrong. And I was suddenly filled with the fear that this time would be the last. I started to cry but I didn't let him see. I needed him to hold my hand more than ever, just as much as he needed me to hold his.

The next morning everything was covered in snow. I couldn't sleep, the beeping and hissing of Daddy's oxygen machine keeping me awake. I got up, put on my coat and boots, opened the back door, and walked outside. The sun was barely waking. A dozen elk gathered in the meadow beside our house, grunting and snorting. I watched them, mouse brown and knob-kneed, bending and shoving their noses under the blanket of snow, searching for life. One mother with a child looked over her shoulder, the breath from her nostrils spilling out into the air. That same cool air filled my lungs. I was so numb. The cold wind gave me the breath that I needed, the sharpness to make me feel. I stood on the porch until my nose started to run and my face began to hurt. I didn't want to go inside. Behind me I heard the door open and my mother's voice interrupted the stillness. I must have looked crazy to her, standing out in the freezing morning air, tears streaming down my face.

"Get in here before you catch cold and I have to take care of you too," she said.

The snow lasted for days, clinging to the earth, refusing to be shaken loose. Daddy's health continued to fade. He could no longer speak. Like an infant he did nothing but sleep. He wouldn't wake up for meals. My mother couldn't even force the food down him. Hospice nurses came and hooked all sorts of new machines to him that made noises to remind us how sick he was. He lost more weight. His arms were thin and sharp. His legs were only bones beneath the sheets, like a canvas draped over tent poles. It hurt so badly to look at him, I

stopped going into his room unless my mother
needed my help to position him in bed. I was
getting sicker too, falling deeper into a depression I
wasn't even aware of. I mimicked Daddy's
behavior. I wanted only to sleep. I didn't study. I
didn't eat. I didn't speak to anyone. I pulled my
bedroom curtains tightly together and refused to
come out of my room, while my mother sat in the
kitchen crying because she was losing both of us.

Soon people I had never seen before were
coming by to visit Daddy. Our house was more
crowded than it had ever been. Each day a dozen
aunts, uncles, and unfamiliar people claiming to be
long lost friends or distant cousins popped in with
baskets of fried chicken and bowls of spaghetti and
cakes and cookies and cheese platters that my
mother and I did not want to eat. They would gather
in my father's bedroom, one or two at a time, and
stare as if he were an exotic animal in captivity at
the zoo. It made me angry. I didn't come out of my
room to say hello to anyone. I couldn't stand them
all huddled together crying, tissues bawled up in
their fists. Even worse were the ones who didn't
cry, but came instead laughing and smiling, telling
stories and pretending everything was going to be
okay, that Daddy would make a full recovery, wake
up, and laugh along with them. Like he had been
playing a horrible joke. Like he would throw the
covers back, jump up from the bed, and exclaim,
"Gotcha!" I stayed in bed and put the blankets over
my face and stuck my index fingers in my ears to
block out the sounds of laughter. "Where's
Jessica?" I could still hear them ask, as if it was
some sort of party or family reunion and I was
supposed to be present. Like I was the hostess. Like

any of them had been invited in the first place. I felt so sick and angry. They were all stopping by our home to do their good deed for the day and I was supposed to be there at the front door with a big smile on my face just waiting to welcome them in to see the dying man. "Come on in! Get a good look! There he is! Touch him one last time! Say your goodbyes now, folks! Today might be the big day!"

Only now do I realize how negative I was. I don't know if my father knew people were stopping by to see him, but he would have wanted them to. He would have been flattered and appreciative of all the people who cared. I resented them all because I knew their presence meant he was dying. I was scared their presence would let death know it was his cue.

My first boyfriend, Andy, had told me about something he called "the death rattles" when we were sophomores in high school. Apparently, every member of his family to die in the last half-century had gotten them a day or two before their lives were over.

"It sounds like they're choking," Andy told me. "This horrible sound comes from their lungs. It's like when you drink from a straw and all the liquid is gone, but you keep sucking anyway. As soon as you hear that, there's nothing you can do. They'll be dead by morning."

I only half believed him. It reminded me of the horror stories my cousins used to tell me when I was a kid, superstitious things about werewolves and vampires that didn't really exist. So, I forgot about it altogether, until I heard them for myself.

On the morning of February 17th, the snow had finally started to melt. Patches of grass poked through the whiteness, and it comforted me to see them. But it terrified my mother.

"I wish it would just stay snowy for a couple more days," she said, nearly in tears. I didn't understand why. My mother hated snow. She despised it. When I was in third grade, she went out to pick up a special Christmas present for my father. Somewhere on highway 15, she hit a patch of black ice. Her car flipped three times end over end. It smashed through the guardrail and collected mounds of earth and dirt and ice along the bumper. The windows shattered. Somehow, she was unharmed. Since then, she hated winter. She watched the weather channel religiously. Even the slightest hint of snow would send her into a frenzy. Now she was wishing for it? I thought being cooped up in the house for so long was finally getting to her.

Classes were in session at the college that morning, though the roads were not completely free of ice. My uncle Lonnie offered to drive me to campus in his truck.

"I've got some business to do in town today," he said, "so I'll just swing back by when you're done and pick you up."

On the ride to school, I was glad that he didn't want to talk about Daddy. He asked me about my classes instead in a vain attempt to break through the heaviness that hung itself around our entire family. He dropped me off at the front door and told me to meet him in the same spot at two o'clock.

I walked into the classroom and only one other person was there. She sat in the back row reading a beauty magazine. I unpacked my books from my bag, took off my coat, and settled into my seat. The professor came into the room, looked at the two of us, then out the window at the icy mountain road.

"Looks like this might be it," he said.

On the drive home that afternoon, my uncle asked me if I would like a part-time job. My other uncle had recently opened a carpet store and was in need of someone to answer the phone. I'd never worked anywhere before and the thought of doing so excited me. He told me they would make some arrangements, and he would let me know when I would be starting. I thanked him for the ride, climbed out of the truck, and waved goodbye. I walked in the front door and saw my mother sitting in the chair crying. The happiness I felt dissolved as quickly as it had come.

"What is it?" I asked.

"If all this snow melts," she said, "and the water rises and the creeks flood all the roads, then…"

"Then what?"

"Then how are we going to get him out of here, if he…"

She started crying harder now. I sat beside her on the arm of the chair and lay my head against hers. Outside the window, the sun poked through the clouds. The snow was receding faster and faster. The big maple tree in the front yard was completely free of it, her naked branches twisting toward the sky.

Later that night while Mom took a long bath, I gathered the courage to go and check on Daddy. Before I even entered the room his breathing arrested me. It was deep and hollow, as if the air couldn't make it through his lungs, but had gotten lost in there, rattling. Daddy's body was bent over in the fetal position, his hips jutting below the blankets, sharp as the mountains outside. I sat down on the spare bed too scared to go closer. Everything was dark except for the bedside lamp, which lit one side of his face only. He looked helpless. For once I didn't want to run away. I sat there in silence for over an hour, the most amount of time I had spent in that room with him in months. I didn't know if he could hear me, but I started speaking.

"I had a good day at school today, Daddy," I said. "I'm learning a lot of new things. And I might be working for Uncle Butch at his carpet store."

I began to cry but I kept talking between the sounds of the oxygen machine and the rattling of his breath.

"I'm glad I decided to come home this semester. I know I probably haven't spent as much time in here with you as I should have. It's just been very hard, you know, to see you sick and everything."

Tears ran down my face, across my jaw, and onto my neck, but I didn't stop to wipe them away. I stood up and sat down beside him on the bed and took his hand in mine. It wasn't shaking this time, but I held it anyway.

His breath rattled and the oxygen machine hissed.

"You've been a very good Daddy to me," I said, barely able to speak now. "Better than I could have ever asked for, and I just want you to know that. I love you more than you'll ever know." I kissed him on the cheek and lay my head against his for a long time. I kissed him again, told him goodnight, and went to bed. Before I was even under the covers, I heard the front door open and my brother's voice.

And then my mother sobbing. It had been less than ten minutes after I told Daddy goodnight. Someone knocked on my door.

I opened it to find my mother standing in the hallway next to my brother. He was leaning against the wall with his face in his hands. She put her arm around me and whispered, "He's gone."

When I was a little girl, one of my favorite things to do was make my father's lunch. He was the night shift foreman of a coal mining company. Every evening after he picked me up from school, I got the cooler out of the back of his truck, took it into the kitchen, and made him a sandwich. He liked bologna the best, with mustard. I assembled the sandwich with love and secured it into a plastic baggie, then placed it into the cooler with an apple, a soda, a few of his favorite chips, and a couple of miniature candy bars, because he always craved something sweet at the end of each meal. But what he loved most was the note that he would find. Each day it would say something new, usually the result of a ten-year-old's brave attempt at writing poetry. No matter what I wrote, I always used the same ending: "I love you more than numbers can count, and numbers never stop." I was very proud of that revelation. The idea that numbers would just go on and on forever without anyone being able to measure or contain them was the best way I could think of to express how much I loved him.

I thought about that the night he died, laying my head on the kitchen table while all of my aunts and uncles stood around me weeping. I had cried so hard I thought that I would die too. Or at least I hoped I would. My mother's sister sat beside me

running her hand along my back. I wasn't allowed
to go into Daddy's bedroom. No one went in
besides my mother and the coroner, a bald man with
dark eyes. I didn't want him to take Daddy
anywhere. I couldn't stand the thought of him being
strapped to a stretcher, shoved inside a hearse, and
driven away into the night, all alone. Didn't anyone
else see that he needed us? He needed us to take
care of him. I would have volunteered to go with
him, to lie right alongside him in the hearse, into the
morgue, into the coffin, into the ground.

They had planned to take Daddy out through the
back door because the stretcher wouldn't be able to
make it up and down the front steps. My aunts took
me onto the front porch so I wouldn't have to see
him being taken from the house. It was colder than I
remember any night being. I wasn't even wearing a
jacket until someone else took hers off and draped it
over me. I looked out at the snow that hadn't quite
finished melting. My mother received her wish. We
didn't speak because none of us had words. There
was no sound except Daddy's wind chimes, the
ones I had bought for him, singing out into the night
air as if to say *I'm sorry*. That sound cut me deeper
than the wind itself. But I couldn't cry any more.

The funeral would not take place until two days
later. There were so many flowers and so many
people. It was so crowded that not everyone could
fit inside the church. Some had to stand outside
without a chance to see Daddy at all. I sat in the
front row between my mother and brother, neither
of us fully present. Daddy had on a blue shirt and
black trousers that we made a special trip to buy for
him the day after he died since he had lost so much
weight. We didn't put shoes on him, just dress

socks, and as he lay there in the coffin, I couldn't
help but worry that his feet would get cold once he
was inside the ground. He looked nice, but he didn't
look like himself. He wasn't wearing his glasses.
His nose looked as though it was made of plaster,
hollow and sharp; a skeleton. His hands were
powdered over and smooth. I held out my fingers
and touched him before I took my seat. He was
cold. It wasn't Daddy.

I heard someone behind me whispering how I
was holding up better than they expected. Everyone
knew how close my father and I had always been. I
didn't cry until my cousin Kathy sang an old
country song called "Daddy's Hands" and I
collapsed into my mother's lap like a child.
Everything after that was a blur. After the service,
the closest family members drove out to the
graveyard in a long funeral procession. Dozens of
cars snaked throughout the winding mountain
roads. I sat in the front seat of my mother's car,
directly behind the hearse. I wondered if Daddy was
lonely in there. I wondered if he was proud, looking
back on all his loved ones spread out across the hills
and valleys, following him to his final resting place.
The snow had melted and it was raining hard. The
floods were coming that my mother had feared,
though Daddy was being buried now high up on a
mountaintop above Homeplace Clinic, in a wild
stretch of rolling bluegrass colloquially called "The
Upper Land", my favorite place to play as a child.
We all sat under a funeral tent in fold-up chairs.
Daddy's casket lay before us, cloaked in fat, orange
flowers.

The casket was closed now. I waited for Daddy
to open the heavy oak lid, crawl out, laugh, and hug

everyone. Then we could all go home. Then we could all pick up where we left off before the cancer went to his brain, before he lost the ability to walk, before he couldn't form words or recognize my face, or remember eighteen years' worth of memories we created together. I kept waiting, but the rain kept falling. My high heels pinched my toes and sunk into the wet earth. I held one of Daddy's handkerchiefs in one hand and a tiny white dove someone had plucked from the flower arrangement in the other. I twirled the dove by its plastic feet, looking deeply into its black, hollow eyes. Someone had glued miniature white beads to its wings. It could not fly, even if it wanted to. I traced the wings with a cold, wet finger while the preacher gave a long, heartbroken prayer. I wished we could both fly somewhere, up over the trees, out of The Upper Land, over Troublesome Creek, deep into the fog that blanketed the mountains, a hundred shades of bruised purple and gray. I wanted to be anywhere else. Any world was better than the one in which my father no longer existed, a world where I was no longer his daughter. I was already someone else, sinking into the mud, holding a dead man's handkerchief, unable to tell whether the water streaming down my face was tears or rain.

After it was over, the prayers and goodbyes were said, and we went home. It hurt being there without him. My aunts, uncles, and cousins had come to our house with food. I didn't want to talk to anyone. I went into Daddy's bedroom, lay down on his bed, and cried until I fell asleep, his handkerchief still clutched in my hand.

***

A lot of time has passed and the grass has finally grown in. For a long time, there was just a mound of dirt in the shape of a casket at the end of your headstone. I sit here plucking the weeds away from the grass. I wipe the dust from the headstone, set your flowers up straight, touching the ground like you're really inside here, like you can really feel my fingers when I place them on the earth, your earth. Everything is quiet except for a few crows that scratch at the trees in the distance, their wings flapping now and again. The gate creaks when the wind blows. I sit here talking for a long time like you can hear me, and I don't know if you can, but I hope so. I tell you about all the things that have passed since I came here last. I tell you I'm back at the university now, that I just turned twenty, that I changed my major to English Literature. I feel you more in the sun that breaks through the clouds in the distance than I do in the earth, and I know that is where you really are. Not here. And I cry for a long time before I stand up and dust off my pants, my eyes blurry and filling up with tears. I lock the gate behind me, say a prayer or two, and make my way down the hill to my car among the falling leaves, the crows never stopping to notice me.

Target

1st Place Poetry Winner   Katherine Edgren

When he came along, my baby brother turned me into a
    a big sister, wanting to keep him safe.

In first grade, while daydreaming, his little burr head
    was slammed in a heavy door by a fellow student.

He got bird poop in his buzzcut
    playing Cowboys and Indians,

suffered a concussion from a hard jar on the ice.
    At a football game, confetti would lodge in his eye.

Later, as a young adult, his neck ached,
    his brain flamed with fever.

It was almost as if he sent out infrared rays sensed by
rattlesnakes
    waiting to strike in the absence of light.

Later, his active mind led him to a Ph.D. in Chemistry,
    provoking him to concoct, spool out, test,

invent and patent advanced coatings
    for extreme environments.   Now, a stroke.

Thrust back to a time before he could ask for water,
    or scratch an itch.

His boat adrift on a lake,
    artillery flashes of lightning overhead.

The Boat Comes In

1st Place Fiction Winner   Arnold Johnston

Dance to your daddy, my little laddie
Dance to your daddy, my little man
You shall have a fish and you shall have a fin
You shall have a codling when the boat comes in
You shall have a haddock boiled in a pan
Dance to your daddy my little man

—"When the Boat Comes In," traditional
Northeast English folksong

At the age of 91 my father was shutting down.
Having him around for all those decades had made
his presence a given in my life. His decline began
with driving, and as the insurance companies
always said, the accident happened within a few
blocks of home.

John Fairbrother didn't like being pushed. He
was on his way to get an oil change, and he'd
stopped at a red light to make a left turn. When the
light turned green, the driver behind him must have
been in a hurry and honked his horn. Annoyed,
John stepped on the accelerator and steered into the
path of an oncoming car. He explained later, in the
Geordie accent his decades in America had never
worn away, "Bloke ahint me tooted, and I just
turned."

I got the call from my wife when I was in the
middle of a meeting at PharmaCom about a new
drug that showed promise for treatment of
Alzheimer's disease. The researchers weren't ready

to turn me and the rest of the writing unit loose on news releases until test results were more definitive, but they did want us to do some articles hinting at breakthroughs to come. Annie taught anthropology at the university, so she could spend a fair amount of time in her home office, meaning she frequently got stuck with John's problems while I was at work.

"I'm really sorry to break into your day," she said, "but John just totaled his new Corolla."

"Jesus," I said. "Is *he* all right?" My colleagues glanced at me with raised eyebrows, then quickly turned their attention to the reports on the conference table.

"He's okay, miraculously. We're at Benson Emergency."

"I'll wind things up here as soon as I can," I said, "and get over there."

"No rush. Really, he's fine. How's it look for the Alzheimer's drug?"

"I forget."

"Bad joke," Annie said.

The irony wasn't lost on either of us, though my father certainly gave no signs of losing mental acuity.

"The cop on the scene wasn't even going to give John a ticket," Annie said. "I told him I wished he would. So he did. And John told me he should maybe quit driving."

"Thanks, babe," I said. "You may have saved some stranger's life, never mind Dad's."

* * * *

On the way home from the hospital John said, "I feel fine, you know. Champion. Maybe I can go back to driving once t'car gets fixed."

"The car's a write-off, Dad." I glanced in my rearview mirror long enough to catch Annie's eye-roll from the back seat. "I'll be glad to handle the insurance settlement."

Ultimately, the three of us agreed that John's driving days should come to an end. I helped make the decision less painful for my always-frugal father by getting the insurance company to settle for pretty close to the original price John had paid for the Corolla.

"How am I meant to get around?" John asked in a last attempt to forestall the inevitable.

I held up a hand. "We'll drive you wherever you need to go, Dad."

John lived in an apartment complex two or three miles from our downtown condo. He'd been unwilling to move out of the apartment, which was really too big for him, after my mother's death three years earlier. Not because of any sentimentality about my mother Eloise, I knew, but because John valued control. The complex catered to elderly residents, but John didn't like being subject to the timetable or the authority of its shuttle service.

John's driving involved not much more than trips to the supermarket, doctor's appointments, and weekend visits to our place to watch baseball or football, and of course the occasional Newcastle United Magpies game on one of the streaming services he'd never think of paying for. Nonetheless, we knew life was going to get more complicated. But what else could we do?

* * * *

Initially, we timed shopping trips for weekends
when I was available or weekdays when Annie had
no classes or office hours. John would trundle
around the market with his own cart and rendezvous
with Annie or me at the checkout counter. Annie
preferred the days when I could join them and help
carry in the groceries. John preferred to shop on
Wednesday, Senior Discount Day. After a while,
though, John decided to give us a shopping list and
stay in his apartment to read or watch television.

"I don't know why they charge me for all these
shows," he'd say about his bare-bones cable
package. "All I watch are the three, what d'ye call
'em, networks. Never bother with all those strange
channels."

Except when you come to visit us, I thought.
Aloud, I said, "I wish you'd get out more. Going
shopping is good exercise."

"Annie does the needful," John would respond.
End of discussion.

So, Annie would dutifully take the penciled
lists, written in John's meticulous old-fashioned
cursive, bring back the groceries and carry them in,
then show him the receipt so he could write her a
check, just as meticulous but in ink.

"I get the feeling he's hoping every time I'll
forget to ask him to pay up." Annie shook her head
ruefully. "Fat chance, after schlepping all the
groceries in."

"I'm sorry I can't help more often," I said with
a frisson of guilt.

"Nothing for it," she said. "You're tied up all
day. And I'm an academic, so I don't really work

31

for a living." This last remark was our running joke about Annie's colleagues, almost all of whom insisted they worked an eighty-hour week.

"At least his lists are easy to read," I said.

Annie laughed. "They can be cryptic, though. His list the other day included muffins. 'What kind?' I asked. He almost did a double-take, then said, 'English, of course.'"

I laughed, too. "I'd like to see him get into that with one of the employees at the market."

* * * *

I would drive over to the apartment complex on weekends and bring John back to watch sports. On the fifteen-minute trip John would keep up a running analysis of other drivers' shortcomings.

"Look at that oud wife," he said on one occasion. "Divena ken enough to signal a change of lane."

I glanced at the other car as it slowed to make a right turn. "Dad," I said. "That old woman is probably younger than I am."

But I knew John's self-image was of the ballroom-dancing Lothario he'd been sixty years ago in England and for several decades afterward when he and Eloise had immigrated to the States with their young son: me. Not that I had ever known my father to stray, or even betray much interest in sex, though one day a couple of months before the traffic accident John had alluded to another "oud wife" in the apartment across the hall who kept inviting him in for coffee.

John had snorted. "I think she's just ettlin to get lucky."

On his visits to our condo, he and I would eat snacks, washed down with beer and an occasional shot of single-malt scotch. Though I'd take a scotch with my father now and again, I never drank the beer, which I stocked especially for John. Avoiding the carbs was one of my own concessions to aging, even though John always eyed my diet soft drinks with disapproval.

"This is champion beer," John said one day, and it was, made at a local micro-brewery. "It's no' Broon," he said, referring to his beloved Newcastle Brown Ale, "but it's no' bad."

"It's readily available," I pointed out. "We get it at the market. You could, too."

John grunted. "If I bought it, I'd just drink it." The beer he bought for himself was Miller Lite, a step up from ditchwater. But it came cheap, in a case of thirty cans, the extra six tinted orange so they wouldn't be missed. And his scotch was J & B. No tempting malt whisky for him, except on weekends.

"This cheese is good and all," John said of our favorite Irish cheddar.

"We get that at the market, too," I said. This brought on another ambiguous grunt.

Annie would usually head off to Macy's while John and I watched the Tigers, the Lions, the Red Wings, now and then the Pistons, and whenever possible the Magpies. Then she'd return, often sneaking her purchases into the house so John wouldn't realize my second wife was such an extravagant woman.

"He likes the way we live," Annie said one day after I had taken John back to his apartment. "And he can afford everything we can. He just can't summon the will to do it."

"Tell me about it," I said. "He never spends an extra dime on himself. Or anyone else."

Annie laughed. "He just can't bring himself to loosen up and enjoy himself unless he's here."

"I guess it's not going to happen now," I said. "Not at his age."

* * * *

"John is so lucky to have Dr. Diefendorfer," Annie said some months later. "With his congestive heart failure and phlebitis he'd likely never have had the last few years to enjoy if Dr. D hadn't been so vigilant about tuning him up."

"I hope Dad's all right at the moment," I said. "He was in a big rush to get to the restroom."

We'd just arrived at Food Waltz, a newly trendy restaurant where we were treating Dad to brunch after a visit to the young doctor who'd been our own family physician for ten years, and who—we were happy to note—was enough younger than all of us to make his being around for the foreseeable future a reasonable bet.

Dr. D's latest diagnosis was that John's pacemaker was working nicely, and that his apparently grapefruit-sized prostate wouldn't be an issue at his age. "More men his age die *with* prostate cancer than *from* it," Dr. D had told us. Of more concern was John's general mobility, exacerbated by phlebitis that would be more dangerous to operate on than leave alone, and by his gradually diminishing kidney function.

"Ready to order?" A rail-thin young waiter with Kohl-lined eyes smiled down at us, pad and pencil poised.

"We're waiting for our guest," Annie said. "He should be back shortly."

"No problem. I'll be back soon, too." The kid grinned, turned on the heels of his earth-friendly shoes, and walked off.

"Nice that we're not causing a problem," Annie said. Food Waltz was located conveniently, but was not one of our favorite places.

"The only problem around here is pronouncing 'scone' properly," I said and got up. "I'm going to check on Dad."

I made my way past murals of babies nestled under cabbage leaves and fields full of other primary-colored vignettes that celebrated organic farming. No pesky pesticides. Nor pesky pests. When I got into the antiseptic-smelling men's room, it gave no sign of occupation save for one stall with a closed door. "Dad?" I said.

"Edward?" John's voice sounded oddly tremulous from the closed stall.

I approached the door. "It's me, Dad. Are you okay?"

"Edward," John said again, as if fixing it in his mind. He went on reluctantly. "I've messed myself. I've peed myself. I couldn't get in here on time."

My heart quickened. This was the beginning of something, I realized. "How about your trousers?" I asked.

"They're okay. Damp. But my underwear's soaked." John spoke each word like the admission of an atrocity.

"Push the underwear under the door, Dad." I got a sheaf of recycled paper towels from a dispenser. "I'll get rid of it."

"I could wash them," John said in a firmer tone, his concern for thrift a lurch toward normalcy. "No need to throw away a good pair of briefs. Maybe you can find a plastic bag."

"Not here, Dad." I wrapped John's sodden tightie-whities in paper towels and dumped them in a waste container. Adult diapers, I thought. We'd need to add them to the next shopping list.

The rest of brunch was somber. Not even the chance to correct the waiter's pronunciation of "scone" could cheer John. "I've told yon fellow before," he said. "*Skahn*, not *skohne*. Then he corrects *me*. They're not really scones, anyway. More like shortcake."

Annie and I exchanged looks. I'd tell her later about the toilet crisis, though I knew her always-sensitive nose had registered the faint whiff of urine.

* * * *

I recognized how humiliated John must feel as the infirmities of age mounted. On another day he admitted that he'd been unable to lower himself slowly onto the toilet seat in our main bathroom. The impact of his weight had caused the seat to split down the middle.

"Don't worry about it, Dad." I put a hand on his shoulder. "You keep track of the Magpies and I'll drive over to VanEyck's for a new toilet seat. I'll have it replaced before Annie gets back from shopping."

"Magpies are like me," he said, "bound for relegation." He was right; the United were about to lose their fourth straight match, this time to the upstart Brighton and Hove Albion side that had recently won promotion to the Premier League.

As I drove to the hardware store, I resolved to step up my own exercise program by including a few more deep knee bends. I bought the new toilet seat; then, before returning home, I stopped at a medical appliance store and bought a lightweight but sturdy foldable toilet-seat frame John could use at home or during his weekend visits. The frame cost a hundred dollars, but I knew better than to expect reimbursement from my father, and I couldn't be bothered with helping him to make an insurance claim. Life was developing enough added complications.

John had always taken pride in his independence and general fitness, even though I had never known him to take exercise other than an occasional walk—his afternoon constitutional around the apartment complex—or lugging groceries in after a shopping trip. Among the family photographs on our bookshelves were two similar shots of John, trim and handsome, one in his British Army uniform, field service cap at a jaunty angle, the other in stylish pleated slacks and sweater, an Ascot at his neck and his hair Brylcreemed to a leathery sheen worthy of Noel Coward. In each shot he was leaning against a wall, one leg insouciantly crossed before the other. Dandyish images of masculine self-confidence.

Thinking of those photographs reminded me of our trip to England the summer after my mother's death. We'd planned to scatter Eloise's ashes, and

had decided on a visit with our relatives, who lived
in the Lake District in Keswick not far from Beatrix
Potter's cottage. We told ourselves the reunion
might help distract John from grief, though he had
reacted to his wife's death with his customary
stoicism. But he was happy enough to join us.

* * * *

We'd landed at Gatwick on an
uncharacteristically hot English day. Discovering
that our four-door Hyundai with automatic shift
wouldn't be available from the rental office until
the following morning, we opted for a night in an
air-conditioned room in the airport's Holiday Inn,
where we availed ourselves of the swimming pool
and later a bottle of good Champagne. Frugal as
always, John took an un-air-conditioned room at the
same hotel and decided to visit some old haunts
from when he'd been stationed in the area during
World War II.

Though he always said his unit had expected an
imminent German invasion, John had described
many more instances of non-military adventures,
always obliquely alluding to various encounters
with women, both young and middle-aged. With
Eloise safely ensconced in the Lake District and
working in a Northern munitions factory, John had
apparently found ample wartime opportunity to
indulge himself, to use the English idiom, as "a bit
of a lad." This hazy personal history was difficult
for me to reconcile with what seemed like my
father's almost fanatically asexual existence over
the past couple of decades.

"Your parents obviously had a sex-life," Annie said. "Otherwise, how do we explain your presence?"

"You're obviously right," I agreed. "But you couldn't prove it by my experience. I do remember hearing what might have been my mother's cry of passion one night from my parents' room in the apartment house they managed in Detroit. But it could just as easily have been her reaction to dropping something heavy on her foot."

"I don't think you've paid enough attention." Annie shook her head at my obliviousness. "He's mentioned enough stuff obliquely to me to suggest he has a past, and not just with your mother."

And, indeed, when John returned from his pub crawl around the environs of Gatwick, he regaled us with a story of how he and a couple of his barracks-mates had been detailed to do some work for a well-to-do widow. She had apparently cooked them meals, and something in his tone in describing occasions on which he'd worked at the house alone made Annie raise her eyebrows at me. On the other side of the ledger, his most vivid and pungently-described recollection—triggered by his stop at a hotel that was still in business—involved his having been stiffed on a bar bill nearly sixty years earlier by a mooching lance-corporal.

"And to make up for it he's been stiffing you on bills ever since," Annie said as we settled in our king-sized bed at the Holiday Inn.

We weren't exactly amazed to see John paying cash for his room the next morning—he couldn't stand the idea of being "in debt" to a credit card company. But driving north later that day in the rented Hyundai, we were horrified to learn that the

cash was coming, not from his redeeming traveler's
checks, but from a money-belt stuffed with around
two thousand dollars. He probably wore it to bed.

* * * *

Finally in Keswick, we settled in a bed and
breakfast place, *The Roses*, where our stifling room
was right next to the street entrance and the late-
returning guests seemed mostly drunk. Meanwhile,
Dad conducted himself like a visiting dignitary in
his sister Ruth's semi-detached bungalow and
treated her ex-miner husband Tom Carricker like an
old family retainer. Ruth's house and our bed and
breakfast quarters featured similar décor, heavy on
Toby jugs, music boxes, flowered wallpaper, and
different-patterned carpet in each room. Fawlty
Towers sprang to mind.
   Much to my surprise, the Carrickers, unfazed by
my father's inflated bearing, held a family gathering
attended by Ruth and Tom's children and their
spouses, as well as their teenaged grandchildren,
and the occasion turned out to be a revelation.
Strong tea was on offer, of course, but so were
Newcastle Brown Ale, whisky, sherry, ginger wine,
and soft drinks for the youngsters; the family also
provided a variety of sweetmeats including trifle,
rhubarb pie, Shrewsbury cake, treacle tarts, and,
yes, scones both plain and currant, pronounced
accurately, with lots of fresh-churned butter and
homemade jam. And as the evening wore on, the
crowded living room of the little house rang with
unaccompanied song.
   Ruth Carricker sang in her clear alto, joined in
harmony by her husband and her daughter Sheena.

"Blow the wind southerly, southerly, southerly,
Blow the wind south o'er the bonny blue sea;
Blow the wind southerly, southerly, southerly,
Blow bonny breeze my lover to me.
They told me last night there were ships in the
offing,
And I hurried down to the deep rolling sea;
But my eye could not see it, wherever might be
it,
The barque that is bearing my lover to me."

I saw Annie transfixed by the unexpected
beauty of the moment, which brought up a flood of
associations from my own recent memory. Before
she died, my mother had requested that I sing "Wild
Mountain Thyme" at her wake, and I had done so,
introducing almost the only sentimental note into
the occasion. I'd sung it again before our arrival at
Ruth and Tom's, when we'd stopped to scatter
Eloise's ashes at the Cumbrian stone circle known
as Long Meg and Her Sisters. And now I sang it yet
again for the family:

"Will ye go, lassie, go,
And we'll all go thegither,
Tae pull wild mountain thyme
All around the bloomin' heather?
Will ye go, lassie, go?"

Annie, always easily touched, was dabbing at
her eyes by the time I finished singing. And then,
without request or remark, John began to sing, in
his rumbling bass, a song he might not have sung
since my childhood in Detroit.

"Dance to your daddy, my little laddie.
Dance to your daddy, my little man.
You shall have a fish and you shall have a fin;
You shall have a codling when the boat comes
in.
You shall have a haddock boiled in a pan.
Dance to your daddy, my little man."

Shocked, I had to excuse myself and make a trip
to the tiny bathroom with its miniature bathtub—
"Not big enough to drown a mouse," as a querulous
guest at Fawlty Towers observed. I stood at the
minute washbasin to rinse the tears from my face
before returning to the party. I'd been quite
unprepared for my father's uncharacteristic
tenderness.

John certainly felt no residual warmth for the
memory of his own long-dead father, from whom
he'd been estranged for most of his life. I abruptly
recalled my four-year-old self standing before a
couple of neighborhood boys on a Keswick
sidewalk. Dressed like me in short pants and
sleeveless Fair Isle sweaters—"jumpers" we'd
called them back then—they'd pointed out a dour-
looking old man with a nicotine-stained handlebar
moustache, wearing a greasy-looking overcoat and
a brown cloth cap pulled down over his thick white
hair.

"That's your granddad," one of them said.

The old man shuffled along the sidewalk and let
himself into a semidetached flat only two doors
down the street from where my parents and I lived.
How could I not have known—or been told—about
the existence of another grandfather in my life?

Stomach fluttering, I'd knocked on the door of the flat, just above the brass plate that bore the name Jas. Fairbrother. When the door finally opened, the old man looked down at me without speaking. For a few moments I stood silently, registering his collarless shirt, the broken veins in his weathered cheeks, and the large pores in his nose.

"I'm your grandson," I finally said. "Eddie."

The old man had stared at me for a moment or two, then jerked his head in what might have been a nod, grunted, and closed the door.

Later, I asked what had caused the estrangement from my grandfather. John's mouth drew down at the corners. "My mother died early," he said. "Cancer. I left school at fifteen and got work on the docks in Newcastle. I turned over my pay to him every week. Then I had a chance for an apprenticeship at an engineering firm. He wouldn't part with the fifty pounds I needed for my fee. So I left and got a room at a boardinghouse in the city. Never spoke with him again."

And when I was ten, and we were living in a Detroit apartment, my father got a Transatlantic call from Ruth, informing him that James Fairbrother had died. By then I knew adults assumed that children either weren't paying attention to their serious conversations, or simply couldn't understand adult matters. But, listening to the one-sided conversation, I realized that Ruth was discussing funeral costs. And my father's definitive pronouncement, which ended the call, was, "Don't expect me to spend a penny on him."

We hadn't been back to England since the trip to scatter Eloise's ashes, and now I could see that John wasn't likely to return except in the same way Mum had found the final embrace of Long Meg and Her Sisters.

* * * *

"How's the Alzheimer's drug shaping up?"

Annie and I had just finished hearing Dan Diefendorfer's summation of my own health—we always attended each other's checkups—and this one had given no cause for concern beyond a borderline cholesterol count, so now the doctor was catching up on my work at PharmaCom.

"The R and D people have run into some snags," I said. "Unacceptable side-effects. But they're still hopeful something will break within the next year or so."

"Too bad they can't come up with something to help John deal with *his* infirmities," Annie said.

"Alzheimer's is one thing," Dr. D said, "but old age is finally just a matter of the machine wearing out. Pumps and hoses and generators. John's had a good long life, and you two have helped keep him as well as can be."

"*You* certainly have," Annie said. "He might have been gone five years ago if you hadn't given him such good care."

Dr. D spread his hands. "It may be time to think about a hospice. I'd recommend *The Arbors*."

"His problems are really just physical," I said. "His mind's sound enough. I've been trying to get him to write a memoir about his younger days. I thought it might help give him a sense of purpose.

44

And I'd like to know more about the past. Before it evaporates."

"Good idea. It'll be good for his cognitive functions." Dr. D stuck out his hand to signal the end of the appointment.

"Who knows if he'll ever do it?" I said. "You can't make him do anything he doesn't want to."

"And time's running out," Dr. D said.

Annie silently touched my shoulder as we walked out to the parking lot.

*　*　*　*

A week or so later we installed a hospital bed in John's apartment and arranged for a visiting nurse. John was no longer able to move around without assistance, and he needed help washing himself, even in his walk to the shower stall. The teak stool in the corner let him sit, but getting him to his feet again was another challenging task.

The nurse, a cheerful Jamaican woman named Sylvie, was helpful. But she often arrived late to John's apartment, and sometimes not at all. I tried to be on hand when Sylvie was there, partly to be of assistance, but mainly to forestall John's saying something outrageous to her. I needn't have worried.

"That poor man," she said in her musical lilt one day when I was seeing her out into the parking lot. "Most of his energy's going just to keep breathing and taking care of business."

When I returned to the apartment, I found John distressed by having "messed the bed," as he put it, speaking with effort. I helped him to the bathroom, which I found more taxing than I'd anticipated,

45

helped him take his pajamas off, and got him into the shower. Cleansing John of shit and piss simply took its place among the array of new tasks that had to be performed. I was touching parts of my father I'd scarcely glimpsed over the decades, let alone laid hands on.

Babies, old people. "As it was in the beginning," I thought. The monotonous human cycle of birth, life, and death, with ours much less unusual than any of us would like to believe. Only what came between the beginning and end had any unique particularity. Ultimately, though, we were reduced to the elemental. Sylvie certainly earned her meager pay.

When I finally got John cleaned and changed, then settled back in the hospital bed on fresh sheets, I drew a chair beside the bed and sat holding his hand, which felt desiccated and papery in my own. All the snotty things Annie and I had said over the past couple of years tumbled in my mind.

I squeezed John's hand, and the old man opened his eyes, Before I formed the thought I found myself saying, "I love you, Dad."

John focused on me for the first time in days. With a breathy effort, he sai, "I love you, too, son." I couldn't remember ever having heard those words from my father. As my eyes blurred with tears, John's fingers tightened on my hand and he rasped, "This is taking too long."

As I sat there feeling the magnitude of the moment, John added, "By the way, you'll find a hundred twenty-dollar bills in a check-box in the top dresser drawer. Don't forget." Then he closed his eyes.

I realized that, however debilitated his body might be, the father I'd always known was still somewhere inside. And I was sure the money belt was tucked away, too, probably still crammed with dollars and pound notes.

* * * *

Two days later, John closed his eyes and stopped talking. His breathing became labored and stertorous. He was, indeed, shutting down.

Annie called *The Arbors*, and to my surprise found that the usually wait-listed hospice was able to find an immediate place for my father. I called an ambulance service and John's transfer from his apartment was accomplished with a measure of care and ease by two linebacker-sized med-techs and a gurney.

Both Annie and I were impressed by the thoughtfulness and solicitude of the staff at the hospice, and by the quiet, cleanliness, and attractiveness of the place, both outside and inside. With its blonde wooden beams, soft lighting, and Swedish modern furniture, it looked more like a Scandinavian lodge than a holding tank for the doomed. Before doing anything else, the staff bathed John, transferring him from the gurney to a pulley arrangement that lowered him into a tank filled with gently moving warm water. I mentally compared this confident efficiency to my own fumbling attempts to clean John in the shower. After the bath, and with a minimum of effort, several *Arbors* staff members situated John in a pleasant sunlit room, where he looked much more at home than he had in the makeshift-seeming hospital bed in his own apartment.

After we took care of the paperwork for admission, the director, a smartly-dressed, attractive woman in her forties, said, "Stay as long as you like. And if you want, we can set up another bed in your father's room." Then she added in a kindly tone, "Of course you've probably been putting a lot of things on hold lately, and you'll want to catch up on those."

As we walked to our SUV in the parking lot, Annie said, "I thought I was a lot better at concealing my expressions."

"Me, too." I poked her arm. "I guess she sees a lot of them."

* * * *

That night Annie and I made love for the first time in over a week, guilty and grateful and desperate. Then we both fell asleep as if we'd been shot with tranquilizer darts.

The trilling of my cellphone roused us both from our deep exhausted sleep into darkness. The phone's timeline showed 4:12 a.m. as I answered the call which was, of course, from the hospice. Beside me in the bed Annie switched on the light on her nightstand and took hold of my forearm.

The soft-voiced woman on the other end of the line identified herself as Virginia Kovacs. When I confirmed my own identity, the woman said, "I am so sorry, Mr. Fairbrother. Your father slipped away a few minutes ago. I check on all our guests regularly through the night, and I try to watch the

48

signs so that family members can be here at the end.
I'm so sorry." She sounded genuinely stricken.

"Please don't feel bad, Mrs. Kovacs. We knew
this was coming. We've said our goodbyes, and he
was ready to go." As I spoke, I registered the irony
of my trying to comfort this stranger at the death of
my father. "We'll be there shortly," I said, realizing
we no longer had to rush.

When we arrived at the hospice, Mrs. Kovacs
was waiting just inside the main entrance. She was
a plump woman in her sixties with a round face
molded into an expression that combined both
sympathy and anxiety. Once again, I reassured her
that our not being present for John's last breath had
done us no injury. Then I went into my father's
room, leaving the two women in the hallway,
knowing that Annie would not want to join me.

John's features were still indisputably those I'd
come to know so well over the decades. But he
didn't look as if he were asleep. He was dead.
Absent. Gone. The neural network that had made
him endearing, whimsical, intransigent, miserly,
formidable, infuriating, was no longer part of the
world, except for what still endured in my own
sparking circuits.

Unable to squeeze out any tears, I touched the
back of my father's cold hand, muttered, "Nothing
more," and went back out into the hall, where
Annie watched me over Mrs. Kovacs' shoulder,
closed her eyes, and nodded twice. She looked
tired, but beautiful, and I felt a tear trickle down one
cheek.

Later, after we'd arranged for death certificates,
selected a funeral parlor, opted for cremation
according to John's wish, taken care of the logistics

of a life come to an inevitable and orderly end, we once again climbed into my Toyota Highlander and sat quietly for a few moments before setting off for home.

My mother had died when Annie and I had been at coincidental professional meetings in Manhattan, I at a palliative care conference on behalf of PharmaCom, and Annie moderating an anthropological panel on ritual practices of Pacific Coast Indian tribes. We'd cut short our meetings and returned to the Midwest. Eloise had been cremated, and John had pretty much left all the arrangements to us, so we'd opted for no minister, no service, nothing at the funeral parlor, just a party at our place with a chance for friends and family to visit and reminisce. James and Alan, Annie's sons from her first marriage, taught at universities like their mother, but they and their families lived so far away and were so busy that I insisted they not try to attend.

And now, thinking of John's leavetaking, I leaned back in the SUV's driver's seat and said, "We need to let Jim and Al off the hook. They have way too many demands on their time at home."

"I suppose you're right," Annie agreed, "though I know they'll feel bad." She frowned. "I wish you were able to keep Rhonda from being there." Rhonda was my ex-wife. "She walked right into our house for your mother's wake and never said a word to me, never even made eye contact."

"But you were the perfect hostess anyway. The hell with Rhonda."

After a moment or two Annie said, "What would John want for a sendoff? The same as we did for your mother?"

"I think so," I agreed. I took her hand. "Poor Annie," I said. "You've been an orphan for a long time. And now you've gotten stuck with pitching in on all of this. I feel as if I've hardly done a thing for you."

"That's ridiculous," she said. "My mother died before we even met. And you were wonderful when my father died—and my Aunt Nellie and Uncle Sam. Don't let me hear you say something stupid like that again."

"Yes, ma'am."

"I can't remember your father ever saying anything about religion," Annie said, looking at me inquiringly. "He seemed to live pretty much in the material world."

I grinned. "John and Madonna," I said. "Interesting combination."

"You know what I mean," Annie said, laughing. "He seemed to look at everything from a purely rational viewpoint. Nothing mystical or metaphysical."

"Not like your Indians up in Vancouver," I said, "that's for sure. We had the religion talk one day when I was in high school. Sitting in the car the way we are now. It didn't last long. I asked him what he thought about God and the afterlife. He said, 'You can believe in magic if you want. I don't.' End of discussion."

* * * *

After the cremation, with less time-pressure than that exerted by traditional observances, we decided to have John's wake on the following weekend, assisted by funeral home personnel and catered by one of our favorite restaurants. "Just as long as it's not Food Waltz," Annie said. The decision gave us time to deal with legal matters and go through John's apartment to decide what to do with his household goods, as well as selecting what we might want to hang onto as keepsakes.

John's will, a simple document written in his beautiful calligraphic cursive, left everything to me. Never eager to spend money, either on himself or anyone else, he had accumulated well over a quarter of a million dollars, mostly in his savings account and several certificates of deposit. We found the check box in the top dresser drawer filled with two thousand dollars in crisp twenties; and, unsurprisingly, in a lower corner of the same dresser we uncovered the infamous money-belt, which indeed still had over five hundred dollars and nearly two hundred pound notes left over from the trip to England. We had picked up most of the travel expenses for the three of us, except on the few occasions when John had "stood treat," as he put it, at occasions involving family and friends, ostentatiously flourishing cash like a visiting millionaire.

"If it's okay with you," I said to Annie, "we'll send five thousand to Ruth and Tom in Keswick. Dad would never have done it, but I know they could use the money. We'll do the same for Jim and Alan."

"It's too bad," Annie said, "he couldn't bring himself to enjoy what he saved. I think toward the end he knew his daughter-in-law would wind up blowing most of it on frivolous things—like us and our kids. I wish he'd spent it on himself. Or Tom and Ruth. Or the boys."

"I think one of the reasons he lived so long," I said, "was knowing he couldn't take it with him. So he decided to stay with *it*."

I turned my attention to a box of photographs, hundreds of crimp-edged black and white pictures and faded color shots, many dating back fifty years or more. Snapshots of my parents and me as a child, English relatives and friends, vacation pictures taken on the shores of Lake Windermere, postcards, old birthday cards, photos and congratulatory cards from John and Eloise's fiftieth wedding anniversary party, which Annie and I had planned and made happen. Pictures of Jim and Alan's graduation parties and weddings, their children and in-laws. An occasional heart-catching discovery, like a portrait of my mother at about ten years of age, one of the few photos I'd seen in which Eloise looked relatively happy, rather than worried. Why had I been so fixated on my father? I wondered, realizing I'd never solve the mystery of my mother's habitually melancholy expression, enigmatic as the Mona Lisa.

I wiped my eyes and forced my attention to the brown paper shopping bag sitting at my feet into which I'd been discarding stuff we knew was, as John would have put it, "surplus to requirements." I was trying to decide about pitching a handful of pictures featuring people I'd either forgotten or only dimly remembered, when Annie said, "You never told me you'd had a brother." Her tone wasn't accusatory, just puzzled.

But she was no more puzzled than I. "Brother?" was the only response I could muster.

Annie waved a piece of paper at me. I set down the box of photographs and took the document from her. Sure enough, it was a birth certificate recording the entry into the world of one Thomas Fairbrother, weighing six pounds, thirteen ounces. The place was Keswick, the parents John Fairbrother, metalworker, and Eloise, his wife. The birth had occurred some seven months after John and Eloise's wedding day. The baby had died some four days later.

"I never knew a thing about this," I said, feeling as if my head were enclosed in some sort of buzzing globe. I set the certificate on the flimsy metal table next to my chair. "He must have died as a result of being premature."

"Six pounds, thirteen ounces?" Annie said. "Pretty sturdy for a preemie. James and Alan weren't much heavier than that, and they're big boys, like you. Maybe it was something else."

A silence stretched between us as we contemplated the likelihood of another familiar story. I finally broke it. "I wonder what other surprises are lurking in the nooks and crannies."

"Well," Annie said, "there's this. It was under the cash box. It looks as if he actually wrote the memoir you were always nagging him about."

She handed me a letter-sized spiral notebook. The cover bore the words, "I Remember." I opened the book and looked at the first page. The graceful handwriting was unmistakably my father's, and the narrative began with an epigraph, a poem by Thomas Hood from which John had obviously taken his title:

I remember, I remember
The house where I was born,
And the little window where

The sun peeped in at morn,

And the tall yew trees so high,
Whose feathery tops would brush the sky.
I remember, I remember.

I began leafing through the early pages, not
really registering a great deal except that my father,
unsurprisingly, wrote clearly and with an eye for
telling detail. I realized that there were, after all,
ways in which I took after him.

"Check the last page," Annie said, her tone
carefully neutral. I glanced at her. She always liked
to know how a book was going to end before she
started reading.

I flipped through the narrative, which was about
thirty pages long, to the final page. Having begun
with his earliest memories, John ended the account
with what he referred to as *his* marriage, a civil
ceremony before a magistrate, without reference to
Eloise, noting that it had endured for fifty-seven
years. But there on the page was the sentence I
knew had caught Annie's eye: "I had been trapped
into a marriage I neither wanted nor could afford."
Another sentence noted that "with the ceremony,
dinner, theatre, drinks at the King's Arms, then the
honeymoon, I spent all my savings."

"Sentimental soul, wasn't he?" I looked at
Annie, who regarded me steadily. "Well, I never
thought it was a match made in Heaven."

I started to lay the notebook on the metal table
when a small loose piece of paper fluttered from
between the pages to the floor. I picked it up and
looked at it. The writing was my father's, but faded

and in a smaller, more cramped hand, the ink faded with age.

"What is it?" Annie asked.

I twitched the sheet in my hand. "Poetry and song are becoming a motif," I said.

"Read it," Annie said.

"It's called 'The Nameless Lass,'" I said, my voice constricted. Then I began to read aloud.

"There's nane may ever guess or trow
My bonnie lassie's name.
There's nane may ken the humble spot
My lassie ca's her hame.
But though my lass is nameless,
Her kin o' low degree,
Her heart is warm, her thoughts are pure,
And aey she's dear to me.
Her heart is warm, her thoughts are pure,
And aey she's dear to me.

"He used to sing it as a party piece," I said, feeling empty and untethered. When I was finally able to go on, I added, "I always thought he was singing about my mother. Now, who knows? The hits just keep coming."

Annie sniffed. "Johnny, we hardly knew ye."

* * * *

After the wake, when everyone else had left, Annie and I sat down in our living room with a half-empty bottle of champagne.

"Nice work, kiddo," I said, raising my glass.

"Nice work, yourself," Annie said, and we drank to that. "Thank goodness Rhonda didn't show up." We drank to that, too.

"I see nobody was tempted by Dad's leftover Miller Lite," I said.

Annie shook her head. "I couldn't even get the kid we hired to pour champagne to take it off our hands. He said it was the same swill *his* father drinks."

"So here we are," I said, "orphans together. It'll be hard getting used to his not looking over my shoulder, literally or figuratively."

"You're not like him, you know," Annie said. "You're loving and generous. And you've forgiven him."

"Forgiven him?"

"For being who he was."

"He wasn't so bad."

Annie poured us the last of the champagne and, raising her glass to me, recited, "Dance to your daddy, my little laddie. Dance to your daddy, my little man."

"I guess the boat has finally come in," I said.

We drained our glasses and looked at each other. Then Annie got up. "I think," she said, "there's another bottle in the fridge."

END

The Lost Quiet

2nd Place Poetry Winner   Jay Kvarnstrom

For years, we walked
among the quiet,
where corn rows
met the trees.

I hopped over ruts
left from spring;
he stepped with care,
beside the mud,
curled, hardened.

It was fall now;
the last leaves clung to branches,
waiting for another frost.

The night before, I'd read
of what was coming,
prepared a final visit,
hoping we'd share the moment—
a preemptive mourning.

I did not know if he'd read of
the imminent dissolution of our peace.

I arrived earlier than usual;
shadows still stretched
into the field,

slipped into their familiar place,
and settled into position.

I waited.

Rows of corn folded into aisles,
sun-dried stalks became shelves,
behind me, the trees
hardened into walls.
The sky above—
fluorescent.

I noticed him from a distance,
and the field, temporarily restored.

I wondered if he also
came to say goodbye,
to reminisce through walks
we'd had among the quiet.

His pace was slower now,
shoulders hunched,
his gaze
extended beyond.

For a time,
silence held the peace
where corn rows met the trees.

It Withers and It Dies

2nd Place Fiction Winner   Adeeb Chowdhury

I sat on the floor with my arms wrapped around my knees, feeling the coolness of the crimson tiles under my bare feet. Freshly sucked lychee seeds lay atop a copy of the *Prothom Alo,* clustered in a puddle of juices that collected ink as they oozed through the thin pages. The sleepy afternoon silence was broken only by the television's dim murmurs and the faint grating of a saw against wood.

"Can you come to lunch tomorrow, Ma?"

Her whisper of a voice almost melted into the rhythmic sawing outside. It was the first thing she had said aloud in some time.

"Yes, Nanu." I hoisted myself off the floor, making my way to the adjoining kitchen. "Yes, I can." Letting the lychee seeds slide off into the trash, I turned a rusty tap and let a stream of water drum onto the steel sink. My palms lingered in its coolness, a brief respite from Khulna's throbbing heat. The dark curls my grandmother had gifted my mother, and my mother me, clung to my forehead. I loved my hair, and I loved that I had gotten it from them. I didn't know if I had ever told them that. But I had a feeling they knew.

As a child, I used to stoop by the door and peek in, hoping to catch a glimpse inside the bustling, steamy, seemingly cavernous kitchen, back when it had been the beating heart of my grandparents' home. The whistling of Calcutta tea kettles and sizzling of over-easy eggs in the morning; the scraping of knives against cutting boards that soundtracked the readying of a family meal; the

hushed, giggling exchanges of local gossip as pots
were scrubbed clean after dinner. Habib Uncle, a
smiling man who always smelled of molasses and
somewhat resembled Bob Dylan with a Khulna tan
— and he leaned into it too, the fluffy-headed
scamp, with his pearwood harmonica that he could
barely even play — used to slip me orange slices
whenever I had tried to peer in.

I could almost still hear it all, even as the
sawing outside grew louder by the minute. The
kettles from Calcutta had been long sold off. Habib
Uncle had died of cirrhosis four years ago.

"Hot day, huh, Nanu?" I returned to the living
room, two glasses of water in hand. My
grandmother responded with a blink and a blank
stare. Her hands gripped the sides of her
wheelchair, the veins running up her forearms
prominent and blue against her graying flesh. Her
upper lip quivered ever so slightly, as if she was
constantly teetering on the precipice of breaking
into tears.

"See, I knew you should've let Umna Auntie
help give you a bath this morning," I chided her,
placing one glass on the floor and the other on the
table next to her. "Just let me know when you want
some lunch, okay? I think the cabbage is almost
ready."

Her orna had slipped down her bony shoulders.
Two decades ago, she would have playfully
wrapped the same shawl around me as I giggled
underneath its soft, checkered canopy of cloth. It
had seemed gigantic back then, like I could get lost
within its green and golden folds, enmeshed within
its faint scent of citrus. Today, it could barely stay
on her shrinking frame.

"Ma," she said finally, speaking up a little over the sound of the sawing. "Can you come to lunch tomorrow?"

My grandmother's Bangla was faint, fragmented, and faltering. She hesitated between words, her crinkling voice briefly trailing off before making its way back; with each pause, I could almost see her eyes dancing aimlessly across the floor, as if grappling for the direction her question had been heading in.

"Yes, Nanu. Of course I can."

She seemed content for a little while.

"Ma," she spoke again. "What is that sound?"

The caustic grinding of steel on wood had indeed grown more aggressive, as if repeatedly catching on something and tearing right through it.

"Nothing, Nanu. Let's turn this up." I reached for the remote to the TV, a thick gray box that made everything on its fuzzy screen look like it was older than the country of Bangladesh. Not too tall a hurdle, given that most of the furniture in this house was. Heck, the house was considered old when my mother's first cries bounced off its walls, and that was the year of the war. The television, five decades and the birth of a nation later, hadn't budged. It was on this screen that my grandparents had listened to the midnight declaration of war as the first tanks began rolling down the street outside; had scanned maps and tracked the continuous fighting to determine when it was safe to get baby formula for my infant mother; had read the name of Nanu's brother on a list of soldiers whose bodies had been identified; had watched as the first flag of independent Bangladesh was unfurled from rooftops nationwide. It was on this screen that my mother had grown up watching Bangla dubs of *Star Trek* and, thirty years later, I watched the English reruns. A series of framed photographs lining the top of the television, reaching across generations and the color spectrum, showed my grandmother, my mother, and me each in our early twenties. If the world around it had changed, the television certainly hadn't noticed.

"How's this, Nanu?" I asked, landing on a channel airing a wildlife documentary. I turned, and my grandmother's eyes weren't on the screen at all.

"I don't like the sound, ma," she whispered. Her gaze was fixed on me.

"Nanu -"

She lifted her hand off the arms of her seat, and I watched its slow, shaky climb to meet mine. The warmth of her colorless grasp was so startling that my wrist almost jerked back in reflex. Her soft palms pressed my fingers into a fist and held it there.

"They're cutting down the tree, Ma."

The last time my grandmother had been able to hold my hand like this, she had still had her smile. It had been a crooked and toothy and pure smile, one that felt like the sun peeking through the clouds just to look at you. It had been a little lopsided to the left, just like my mother's and mine.

"They're cutting down your tree. You live there, Ma."

But time had changed her face. Her skin sagged as if slowly melting off of her skeleton. Her eyes, perpetually glazed over in silent exhaustion, drifted to the floor even as she faced me. Her lips were pursed in a tight, thin line.

"They have to, Nanu. They need the space."

The sawing lacerated the air with its unruly, arrhythmic screeches. Barbaric. Unnatural.

"No," she said simply, her voice straining ever tighter. Her hand, clasped around my fist, shook to and fro. "No, it's your tree, Ma."

"It's okay, Nanu." I reached for her other hand, but she squeezed the arm of her wheelchair in a quivering grip that drained all color from her wrist. Her mouth crumpled, and she began blinking profusely. I grabbed her head and pressed it against my stomach just as she released her bated breath in a hauntingly unfamiliar cry, a sound I had never heard her make. An almost animal sound, wrenched from her lungs and strangled by heaving sobs. I slipped my fingers into her hair, staring at the wall as her face trembled against my ribs. "It's alright."

The sawing seemed to have grown deafening by now. It was impossibly loud and ridiculously close.

"Tell them to stop, Ma," she begged, her words almost swallowed by choked whimpers. "You live there."

I refused to take my eyes off the wall. She pulled aimlessly on the sides of my shirt as the sawing dug into our ears, refusing to subside.

"I don't live there, Nanu. No one does."

The sawing cut into my head, my neck, my chest. I wrapped my arms around Nanu's face. The blades couldn't get to her.

"You live there, Ma."

The horrible screeches crescendoed, enveloping us in the unforgiving wailing of a tree being gradually torn from limb to limb. The sawing was now screaming — piercing death cries that rattled the windows.

"Ma," she uttered, but the rest of her words were cut off by a deafening, noiseless snap that plunged the world into momentary silence. For a vanishing moment, every sound stopped. The hollow, lifeless thud that came after sounded distant and decisive.

I cradled my grandmother's head, listening to the sobs seeping out of her body.

*

I sat on the soil with my arms wrapped around my knees, feeling the coolness of the grassy dirt under my bare feet. In the subdued moonlight, the garden looked black. The leafy canopy I used to disappear into had been razed, the old specters of my childhood lurking among the headless stumps scattered around me. The winding gravel pathway my grandfather had carved with his bare hands now belonged to weeds, vines, and debris. The single lamppost in the dead center of the garden, long robbed of its humming glow that had illuminated so many of our nighttime walks here, was barely visible in the darkness.

Against the moonlight, the dead mango tree was a looming sentinel, a leafless cadaver towering above the other occupants of the garden. Its lower branches had been amputated, including the one that had been sawed off this afternoon. Its lifeless husk of which looked like it had already begun its slow, rotting descent into the dirt. I hadn't spoken to the developers in some time, but I figured the rest of the tree would be gone by the end of June. Half the garden already was.

Even in the dark, I could see the shallow, grainy patch in front of the tree where my mother's grave had been. We had been given about a month to

exhume her remains before the developers began
their work. If we had known we would have to sell
the property so much sooner than expected, maybe
we wouldn't have buried her here in the first place,
although I had been trying not to dwell on that
thought too much. I wished we could've kept her
here longer. At least until she had melted into the
soil and there was nothing left to dig up and haul to
a cemetery, she had never set a living foot in. For
what it was worth, she had been buried at the base
of the tree for most of Nanu's decline, so she hadn't
had to see the worst of it. She had left under the
impression that her own mother still knew who she
was.

The sandy patch seemed bizarrely small, like a
grave for a child. How my mother had ever slept
there was beyond me. I almost felt the need to
apologize for the discomfort. *Sorry, Ma, we
should've dug a bigger hole.* But I liked to believe
that for her, it was like coming home. She was, after
all, back under the tree whose branches she used to
swing from as a child, her little feet scraping the
very same dirt and soil. My grandfather used to talk
about the tree as if it were the house's sibling —
"They grew up like this," he would say, holding up
two fingers pressed firmly together -- and it felt
only right to call it family. My mother had been
buried with family.

I lay my hand where she had been. I wish I
could say I felt something — some warmth, some
stirring, a disembodied heart beating deep in the dirt
— but the ground was cold, dry, and dead. As if no
one had ever been there at all.

I'll be back, Ma. I didn't know if I said that
aloud. But I had a feeling she knew.

The house was dark apart from a single window illuminated by rapidly flickering colors. As I slipped into the living room, leaving the door ajar behind me, the murmurs of the television were almost imperceptible. Nanu sat in her rocking chair as it rolled to and fro, her head bobbing along with it. Her chest ballooned with each breath and sank with each whistling exhale. Her dozing face was cast in the alternating green, orange, and pink of the television's pale glow. The February issue of *Prothom Alo,* the same edition she read every day, had slipped out of her fingers and lay face down on the floor.

I sat down next to her, her hand dangling inches from my face. The television was on the same news channel she used to watch with my grandfather every night until one of them was snoring away. My mother used to tell me how she wasn't supposed to watch the news until she was older, and how this had only encouraged her to sneak in and watch from the floor whenever both of them had dozed off. She now watched me do the same from her picture on top of the television, tucked in between her mother and daughter. In the room's dimness, one could be forgiven for thinking we were the same young woman who had been excused from ageing for half a century. Our flowing black curls framed our angular faces and rested on our shoulders, slightly pinched together the same way. Although I had seen neither in a long time, our smiles looked the same, too: the toothy grin that was a little lopsided to the left.

"Ma."

The snoring had stopped. Nanu's hands stirred next to my face.

"Go back to sleep, Nanu. I'm sorry." I rose to leave. She raised her hand, stretching out her empty palm, and I paused.

"Have you had dinner, Ma?" Her voice was low and groggy.

"Yes, Nanu."

"Will you sleep soon?"

"Yes, Nanu."

She fell silent. Her palm was quivering. She looked at her outstretched hand for a moment, then raised her head, meeting my eyes. I placed my hand in hers, and she closed her fingers around it.

"Do you know my name, Nanu?"

She continued staring at my hand in hers. Her orna had once again slipped down her shoulders. In the fleeting colors of the television, she looked white, then red, then green. Her brow creased as she seemed to study the top of my hand, running her thumb gently along my skin.

It's okay. I didn't know if I said that aloud. But I had a feeling she knew.

"Ma," she said finally. "Can you come to lunch tomorrow?"

She opened up her fingers. My hand didn't budge. I wanted to soak in the warmth of her palm for as long as I could.

"Yes, Nanu. Of course I can."

From my angle, it was hard to tell, but it almost looked as if she smiled. It was a little lopsided to the left.

Lament for the Loss of a Poetry Section

3rd Place Poetry Winner   Kenneth Boyd

It was hard to find poetry books
even traveling to a locally-owned store
that might have poetry, even a chapbook,
that wasn't popular, emotional fluff
or a reprinted triage of words
fraught with sophistry and poetry therapy,
certainly no treatment of free verse expression.

The store's façade was painted
like a cartoonish wall of books. I entered
to a bell choir. Still, I walked around defenses
of a maze of shelves to the back of the store
and the smell of postmortem paper.

Not there, not anywhere, I sighed.
Poetry wasn't a dedicated section
somewhere near, anywhere to be found.

There were old books—gifts inscribed
to friends, snooty bookplates like deeds,
spines with Dewey Decimal band aides
and prices penciled tragically on front
free end papers. Some claimed,
"first editions," lacking bibliophile
authority, on mixed-up, makeshift shelves.

There in a soliloquy, while browsing,
I lost hope, but looked to the books,
How are we to make choices?
How are we to know love and forgiveness,
the difference between beauty and blighted
stains, loss and gain, contempt and grace,
a heartfelt embrace or a breach of faith?

Even the wall of books looked fallen, missing
their poetic companions, offering only tears
of dust. They were in no rush to leave home.

Lured by an unexpected score, I paid the price
and exited, exposed by the announcement
of those busybody bells.

At least, under the sunlight, I photographed
the Three Lions Fountain in the square, so I left
with a souvenir—a megabyte of pointless
memories and three free bookmarks to mark
the startling genius of a poet's mind.

Mythic Muse

3rd Place Fiction Winner   Sonali Kolhatkar

The computer screen taunted him. A blue-white canvas, unchanging and defiantly blank.

He typed a few words. Hit delete. More typing. Delete.

Kavya had engaged in such futile exercises for hours, for days, and truth be told—in spite of the claims he made to his agent and publisher—for months.

At present, he found himself far from his Hollywood home, on the beachy outskirts of Gokarna, Karnataka, a little-known town on India's southwestern coast, rife with rich mythology, and home to a towering statue of Lord Shiva rising a hundred and twenty-three feet into the sky. His cabin overlooked one of the most isolated and breathtaking coastal landscapes of the Indian subcontinent. A stunning private beach. A secret lair for top-tier writers and artists.

The two-week retreat was his publisher's lavish outlay, a desperate ploy to birth

Kavya Shaw's follow-up bestseller from the gestative confines of his brilliant mind. But now, as he sat at his writing desk with a view of the water, his delete button remained disconcertingly overused.

When his agent had pleaded for a first draft, or even an outline, Kavya had insisted, smacking fingertips against greying temples, "I have the story, up here! I just need peace and quiet to write it down."

As the sun set on his first night in Gokarna, with nothing but "peace and quiet," and a dazzling half-moon rising through a cloud-soaked sky, Kavya's finger hovered over the keyboard for a long moment. On a whim, he typed "Once upon a time…"

He laughed hysterically into the still cabin air and smashed his finger against the delete button until the cursor could move no more and all he could do was keep silent vigil for words that never came.

A thick sigh—the perpetual soundtrack of his empty screen—harmonized with the ebb and flow of ocean waves outside. He stared through the window at an expanse of foam-tipped azure as far as the eye could see.

A head bobbed in the moonlit water, and he sucked in his breath.

A porpoise? Or perhaps, a dolphin?

There it was again. The hairs on his arm rose and he stood up to peer at the choppy waters. Someone was unmistakably swimming, and yet the illuminated sand was pristine and footprint-free. The figure rose through the water and waded onto sand. It was dressed in white and moved like a woman's body.

A black cloud slipped over the moon, and the beach blackened momentarily. When moon rays lit the vista seconds later, there was only empty water and sand. He blinked, disbelieving. Had he imagined her?

That night he fought his bed clothes in a fitful, and ultimately unsuccessful, effort at sleep.

The next morning, he made his way down to the water. He was alone and swam until his feet no longer treaded sand. Tall cliffs rose up protecting a bay verdant with coconut palms.

The afternoon turned into evening, and he ate a meal, and still, the blank screen stared back defiantly. By sunset he stared through the window, half expecting the buoyant apparition to reappear in the water, but there was nothing.

* * *

Kavya had desperately hoped the painstakingly crafted prose of his first book would make a splash somewhere in the obscure annals of the literary world. But unexpectedly, it snagged the Booker Prize and blew up and now it was everywhere.

He was bombarded by interviews, appearances, book club endorsements, blurb requests, guest lecture invitations, and book signings, living every writer's dream. The book sales rendered him so wealthy he no longer needed to work his 9-to-5 job at the Los Angeles Times. So, he quit, purchased a brand-new home in the Hollywood Hills, and hired an Instagram-famous decorator to curate the perfect writing studio so he could work on his follow-up bestseller.

But no words came forth. Kavya Shaw, breakout literary star and erudite intellectual had no idea what to write next.

The frenzied waterfall of ideas he had distilled into the first book during late-night writing sessions, while working a full-time job, had dried into nothingness. His peers, jealous of his unlikely success, had slapped him on the back with pronouncements of *I can't wait to see what you'll do next.*

But next was nothing. And now, on this haunted beach, a ghost lurked in the waters, taunting the hollowness in his head.

* * *

A week passed and, still, Kavya had nothing to show for the expensive writing retreat other than five empty bottles of wine and a cluttered sink, brimful of debris from prepared foods delivered every few days.

He felt a pull, not to the story he couldn't write, but toward the window, and the distant collage of alabaster cream, piped artfully over a sapphire spread and the mysterious figure that haunted his dreams.

The sun marched evening-ward and Kavya stood and kicked his stiff legs, urging blood to flow down limbs. A dozen jumping jacks pumped his body and mind. "Tonight, will be the night," he said out loud, panting and sweaty.

A new night, a new pledge. The story will come. I can feel it.

He ate silently, watching darkness plunge the valley below into secret shadows. The moon only the previous week had been half-full and bright as a spotlight, its fractured shards reflected in the churn of violent waves as though inaugurating his retreat. Now, it was new and hidden from view. A subdued tide revealed itself by the dim glow of starlight.

An impulse possessed Kavya. He would write by the water's edge, ensconced in warm sand. The words would flow out of him like the relentless roil of the sea upon land. He pulled on sneakers, shoved a notebook and pen into his back pocket and snapped the emergency headlamp onto his forehead.

His foot slipped for an instant on the smooth rock steps outside his cabin and he cursed, grabbing the wooden railing to steady himself. In the dark of night, the familiar beach was an upside-down echo of its sun-drenched cousin. As his feet hit sand, bite-sized albino crustaceans scurried into pencil hole homes by the beam of his headlamp.

The sand was smoothed by an even drenching and Kavya's footprints were the only indentations visible alongside minuscule crab holes. He breathed in salted wind sloughing off the surface of softly lapping water and walked further out, toward the retreating skin of low tide.

This would do.

Legs crossed and notebook illuminated, his nib hovered over a page as blank as the untouched beach. Minutes passed and no great thread of story emerged, no pithy first line, no kernel of craft or story seed. He was doomed to flail under the weight of grand expectations, to burn out like a fiery supernova.

He sighed, switched off the headlamp and closed his eyes to meditate. An

unmistakable echo of breath reached him—
not from his own chest but from the water.

Every hair on his body stood on end,
magnetized by fear.

There was someone in the water, in the dark
heft of night, inside the sinking swirl of
water, there was, assuredly, another person.

A scream caught in his throat as the
breathing, regular and pulsing, came nearer.
The sharp exhales of a swimmer. Kavya's
body was paralyzed, but his eyes danced in
a frenzy, this way and that, into the
darkness. Too terrified to inhale lest he alert
the monstrous breather, he began to tremble.

Then, adrenaline surged and he snapped the
headlamp on, flooding the scene before him
into blinding brightness. Skin illuminated,
dark hair slapped and flapped, a white sail
whipped his face and he went berserk with
panic, falling onto his back, his notebook
flying through the air before it landed with a
thwack somewhere out of reach. Kavya's
throat stuck and then unstuck and he
shrieked a high-pitched ragged tear of a
scream.

His limbs flailed against sand, and distinct footsteps pattered close by, sending grit sprinkling into his eyes and mouth. He coughed and spat and swirled his head in wild panic. The light swung this way and that as he turned away from the water. Shafts of light cast sand and rocks into relief. A swish of white in the distance disappeared into a large rocky outcropping at the base of the hills that ringed the private beach.

"Who's there?" he yelled, the bellow of his own voice anchoring him to the desolate black beach. He stood, readjusted the headlamp, and planted his legs into a fighting stance, ready to tackle the ghost. For it had to have been a ghost. The sandscape, moments earlier, had shown no markings, no bi-pedal indentations, but his own. Now, there was a second set of prints.

Kavya steadied his breathing to slow his racing heart and surveyed the snow-angel mark of his tumble in the sand. The wraith's prints had come within five feet of him and he shivered in the humid ocean air. He picked up his notebook, dusted sand off, and briskly clambered back up the stone steps to his cabin, glancing back to ensure there was

no pursuer, and locked himself inside,
panting and doubled over against the door.

Something, someone, was out there. An icy
chill crept up his skin and he scratched his
forearms and thighs as though the hairy legs
of phantom insects scrabbled across them.

* * *

An uneasy sleep marred by nightmarish
glimpses of skin against white gauze left
him sluggish in the morning. He shivered
and sipped hot coffee as the sun rose outside
his window. Below, the sand beckoned
examination.

By midmorning he descended to the banks
of the Arabian Sea. The sand-angel lay
innocuous and fading as wind blunted it
beyond recognition. Had it been a dream?

No, last night's footsteps of a barefoot
wraith led to the rocks ringing the bay. He
had indeed encountered another.

He followed, mesmerized. The tide was high
now. Waves crashed onto shore, rising ten
feet into the air, compensating for the calm
of the previous night. Into the intermittent

battering-ram sounds of salt water, a reedy
melody pierced.

Kavya faltered, but continued walking,
slower this time, ready to bolt in spite of the
bright inoculation of sunlight against
nightmares.

The melody filled the air, a woman singing
on the wind, her voice plaintive, heart-
rending. He did not understand the words
for they were likely sung in one of the
myriad local dialects common to the
Karnataka coastline. The voice was
sandpapery but tuneful. A husky ode to…
what?

Within the outcroppings, folds of layered
black rock insulated the air. Here, it was
warmer, quieter, protected from the walls of
slamming water. The song filled his ears, the
magic of a minor key weaving its way
through his pores, slipping under his skin.

There she was, a specter dressed in layers of
white wrapped against dark skin, a lilting
tune scraping out of a lithe throat. Her eyes
were averted and her head leaned to one side
as she sat against a smooth rock, braiding a
basket of palm leaves with quick-moving

fingers, a slight frown of concentration grooved into her forehead.

He could have sworn he heard the air crackle. She shunted her gaze sharply upward at him but continued singing. Fingers stilled and dark eyes squarely bore into his, voice still ringing, still scraping against his heart.

Kavya gasped in horror. One side of her nose was badly mutilated, roughly chopped off and grotesquely healed. Her nails were long and sharp, blackened like the talons of an eagle.

The ascending notes needed reconciliation. To stop midway would have left the song uncomfortably unfinished. He recognized her need to finish, to balance the scale, and he paused, indulging the ghost its song.

And then she was silent. Her face was striking, even with a maimed nose. A luxuriant black braid draped down her back and thick eyelashes girded deep-set eyes. Dark hollows against her cheekbones suggested recent anguish.

Their gazes locked. A writer and a ghost.

"Hello," said Kavya. "Do you speak English?"

She said nothing but stooped, then raised herself up, half-finished basket in one hand and a clutch of dried leaves in the other. She sighed, stared at him and turned on her heels to walk further toward the rocks, glancing back to see if he would follow.

Kavya hesitated, then trailed, keeping his distance.

A cave within the rocks was transformed into a living space, a shaded, snug abode with a ring of stones sporting remnants of a fire. Next to it lay a jute-rope cot, a terracotta pot covered with palm fronds that presumably held fresh water, and a small store of food: baskets of coconuts, bananas, and salted fish, a few jars and spoons.

The phantom in white squatted and lit a fire, expertly wielding a matchbook to light newsprint—the only evidence of outside influence within the wild hermitage—and stoke wood. She placed a battered saucepan over the fire, poured several cups of water from the pot, and added a handful of dark leaves as the water began crackling up the edges of the pan.

Tea. She was making tea.

Kavya sat on the sand awaiting her attentions. She hummed an abrasive tune, an echo of her earlier song, and poured hot, dark liquid into two chipped clay cups.

She approached him and his heart thudded wildly as he wondered if she would walk right through him. But she bent close, handed him a cup and sat across from him with her own cup in hand, sharp fingernails tapping against the clay.

"Sorry I don't have milk," she said, eyes locked onto his, as she sipped.

She spoke English. The rough voice was slightly nasal, likely the result of her disfigurement, he realized.

"It… it's okay," he stammered. "I'm Kavya Shaw. And you are?"

The dark-skinned woman wrapped in white stared at him as though scouring his face for traces of familiarity.

"Minakshi," she said, offering nothing more.

"I see. I'm a writer. I've been staying at the cabin, and I thought there was no one else here."

Silence.

"That was *you* last night, swimming in the dark?" he asked. "And before that, a week ago."

She said nothing but lowered her chin in acknowledgement. Then, she asked, "What are you writing?"

The question was heavy. She likely knew nothing of world-renowned Kavya Shaw, the wild popularity of his debut novel, the accolades and awards, record-breaking sales, or the high-stakes follow-up book everyone expected him to write. The weight of *What are you writing?* lay upon his chest like an anvil.

The tea was strong and burned bitterly down his throat. "I'm still working out the story," he lied. "Tell me about you, Minakshi? Who are you and why do you live in this cave?"

"I am sister of Ravana, King of Lanka," she said, her voice like the crunch of dead leaves underfoot.

King, who? Karnataka had no modern-day kings as far as he knew. There were some royal families in northern states like Rajasthan, but this far south?

Minakshi smiled and a face that was clearly once beautiful, transformed into a macabre relic of a skull, ancient and terrifying. Kavya flinched.

"A long time ago," she continued, "I fell in love. But Rama was already betrothed. I begged my brother to release my lover from his promise to another, but he remained beholden to the greater good." Her dark eyes pierced his perplexed face. "Let me start at the beginning," she added.

She was named Shurpanakha at birth, and when she came of age, a man who was mortal enemy to her brother Ravana, raped her. Forced into marrying her rapist to hide the stain on her family's honor, a great war was fought over the illicit union. Ravana's wife, her kind sister-in-law, saved her from certain death at her brother's hands and she lived her days as an ascetic, vowing to wear not a single stitch of clothing other than the gauzy cotton sari she was currently wrapped in.

"It was then that I met Rama," she whispered, tears filling the corners of her eyes.

Hours passed and she spoke and spoke. The diffuse sunlight illuminating the cave waned. Still, Minakshi shared her story, a mesmerizing, scratchy account of love and tragedy.

Kavya's mind slipped into her tale with ease. He hung onto every word, saw the world through her eyes. A jungle's tangled vines and riotous flora. Wild monkeys wielding arrows and swinging tails on tree branches.

Shurpanakha's lover, Rama, a bright-eyed, smooth-faced man, God incarnate, with whom she consummated her vows in a cave not unlike this one. Her lover's brother, Lakshman, who conspired with her own brother Ravana to punish her permanently.

When Ravana held her down as Lakshman cut off her nose to ruin her, she swore she would not shed a single tear. When she hid in these caves, turning to the healing waters of the sea to repair her wounds, she renamed herself Minakshi. Her tale touched Kayva so deeply, he wept.

"And your lover, Rama? What did he do?" asked Kavya, his voice cracking from disuse. "Were there no sympathetic people to help you?"

"It is late," she said. "You must go."

Kavya blinked and looked around. The small fire had continued to burn, seemingly powered by the oxygen of Minakshi's story. He shook his head to clear his thoughts.

His thoughts. His head was full. Full of threads, tangled and begging for clarity and expression. Stories, dozens, hundreds, bursting through every seam in his skull.

"I have to go," he agreed.

Minakshi stood. "They will be here soon," she said, as he trotted into the dark, with only the thinnest moon sliver to guide him

back toward the beach and the steps leading
to the cabin.

Who will be here soon?

He hadn't thought to bring the headlamp for
there had been bright daylight when he left
the cabin that morning. Now, he foundered
through sand and felt around for the stone
steps in the pitch darkness and stubbed his
toe.

A curse escaped his lips just as a low hum
became audible. Kavya looked around, and
in the distance, on the opposite bank, an
orange glow moved through the cliffs. Not
one, but several pinpoints of light, flaming
torches held aloft by many hands. They
were rapidly making their way down.

He stumbled up the stairs, grabbing a hold
of the wooden railing for balance and
guidance. Up, up, up, panting with effort
and fear. The hum of chants and shouts
echoed loud. A clear, high-pitched voice
emerged from the rocks, cutting through the
throng's buzz. Minakshi was singing her
song. It was bolder now, a siren warning, a
signal to the mob that she was alive and
unafraid.

Kavya's heart rammed into his chest, alarms ringing inside his head as the mob grew deafening. They were on the beach now, feet slapping on sand. He struggled to open his cabin door and slipped inside and slammed the door shut. The sounds of the mob and one woman's song of power dampened through the walls encasing him.

He sat at his desk and opened his laptop. It powered to life, its blue-white light illuminating fingers hovering over keys in the dark.

He hesitated. Minakshi's song was louder now, more urgent and defiant. The mob would surely be upon her. He ought to help. Perhaps call the authorities.

But there were words now, appearing as though by magic, flowing from his fingers and into the blankness, filling it with a story, an epic of great significance, a tale to rival any he had ever written.

Minakshi's words had broken the dam, and now a relentless torrent flowed so fast, he had to swim for his life or risk drowning.

He wrote and wrote. Shouts and song
tapered into the thrum of ocean. Night faded
into pink dawn. And still, Kavya wrote, his
fingers aching, wrists crying out for rest.
But the spark burned feverishly bright.

Nothing would diminish it now. Not even an
abrupt end to the rasping song of his muse.

October Full Moon Special

Home of the Brave

Kate Tell

this is a land that was not made for me.

an earth that has fought me since i was born,
at every corner, pushed me to the brink
to see if i will even want to stay.

if i can stay.

i feel the world is sitting on my chest,
crushing my ribs and cracking down my spine
and when i gasp for air it tells me that

this is what i deserve.

i walk fast upon the dirt as it breaks,
hurriedly and running from what follows,
worried that i have been losing myself
but never turning 'round to see for sure.

this is a land that was not made for me.

i wake up wrong, and wish i hadn't slept.
i stretch wrong, and find my bones hurt more,
too.

i talk wrong, and wish i had never spoke.
i walk wrong, cry wrong, fuck wrong, sing
wrong, and

i learn wrong,
write wrong,
*i do everything the wrong way and then wonder
why
everyone's better.*

this is a land that was not made for me.

to mom and dad and brother: please don't cry
just as i have always cried for you.

this is a land that was not made for me.

their eyes are black by what has come before.
they blink and wonder why they deserve this,
why they earned such stinging pain and hatred,
the men will crumble to their knees and scream,
while women dance until their hearts give out,
and children do not even know to cry.
those in between will call their life a lie.
the world was never meant to end in flame
or ash or ocean tides that swallow worlds
and homes and the place that we call our own.

the world will end in quiet crumbling.

this is a land that was not made for me.

so i will destroy it myself.

i'll rip dollar bills til the blood it spills

reaches my ankles. i will smash my fists
against the skyscrapers until they touch
the Hudson's floor. i'll laugh so loudly and
purely over coffee that it will
shake evil to its core.
i'll love those who deserve it so much so
that i, too, will overshadow the sun.
i will dance with everyone watching now.
i'll kiss and cry and eat while being seen,
as my brain bursts out from the inside,
bulging my eyes, loud pops in my eardrums,
cursing me for even having the guts
to exist in this way,

"how stupid could you be? why would you dare
to do this? you are one in billions
and yet
you have the
audacity
to believe?"

and i will look backwards,
facing the mountains i have built out of the
hatred i have harbored
and the oceans of darkness that i have loved with
all of my heart,
and i will feel only pity.
my heart will no longer yearn for quiet,
for silence,
for death.
it will see the days spent at the peaks and have
only regret.
it will see the nights spent out at sea and pray for
forgiveness.

this is a land that was not made for me.

so i woke up and lived in one that was.

HUMAN REMAINS

Cynthia Close

His ashes arrived yesterday in a cardboard box labeled HUMAN REMAINS. The letters were all in caps, over 3 inches tall. Impossible to avoid. It seemed almost sacrilegious. As if he was naked, his essence exposed. I knew the USPS was the only way to legally ship ashes, either human or animal, in the United States. No other service, not FEDEX, UPS or other courier can be used. That's the law and it's what the director of Lemon Bay Funeral Services told me back in 2015 when I had my mom shipped in a granite urn from Englewood, Florida, to me in Burlington, Vermont.

The law is not negotiable. It seems to be supported by commercial shippers despite the fact they lose a seemingly endless source of income. The USPS has specific guidelines "to respectfully ensure their safe handling." I wonder what goes through the mind of a postal worker whose responsibility it is to get these last vestiges of what was a life to their destination. But it's not a "final destination." It's more of an interim sort of thing, a dilemma that I now have. Perhaps I should have coughed up the extra cash to have him interred at Mount Auburn Cemetery, witnessed by those who knew him, but he'd already cost me, and I harbored a resentment that interfered with the energy it would take to organize such an event.

Ritchie would've preferred his body be laid out to rot, naturally, somewhere in the wooded area surrounding Fresh Pond Reservation in Cambridge, the city he most loved and where he lived his entire adult life, save for a year spent on a radical artists commune just outside of Vienna, Austria. God, religion, spirituality or any notion of an afterlife were of no interest to him. They were also of little interest to me. Until now.

Thunderstorms are moving in. The room darkens as I write this sitting in my kitchen that also serves as a make-shift office where I write and most recently have made tentative gestures towards making art again. The red, white, and blue Express Mail package from the Keeffe Funeral Home has been sitting on a table in my entryway for the past three days. It is unavoidable yet I avoid it. Writing his obituary the day he died was easy. I'd been writing versions of him and painting versions of him at various times throughout the 43 years we'd known each other. We met in 1983 and lived together off and on until I finally left him in 2011.

It was a gut-wrenching tear-your-heart-out-face-to-face kind of leave taking. I knew I had to go. He stood frozen, immobile, nearly catatonic. Did he say anything in our last moments facing each other in the driveway of our now empty condo, swept clean for the new owners? The last bit of what we'd had were embodied in our dog, Jasper, who sat motionless on the asphalt halfway between us. His regal, German Shepard-like countenance acted as a magnetic pole, holding us in stasis. He was our most recent rescue pup. We shared a love of dogs. Almost inaudible, Ritchie choked on his words. "I thought you were taking the dog." We'd barely spoken to each other these last few weeks. He tried to pretend it wasn't happening. "Do you want the dog?" I asked, thinking he has nowhere to go and having the responsibility of a formidable looking dog would not make finding an apartment any easier. My heart was crumbling, not sure how he'd answer. I imagined he'd give in at the last moment. But he didn't. He'd ignored the fact our home had sold and that we could no longer sustain our Cambridge lifestyle on my retirement income. Our mutual friend and fellow dog lover, Alka, had driven over to help escort Ritchie somewhere else. I had no idea where that somewhere else might be. Ritchie started to cry. I had never seen him cry before. "Yes…" he stammered. In that moment, Alka, who had not said a word but patiently bore witness to the death of our relationship opened the car door. Jasper bounded in the back and Ritchie slid into the passenger seat. They took off. Although I can clearly see this moment as if it had been the final scene in an Academy Award-winning movie, I can't remember what I did next.

I've always experienced life as an observer. I see and feel myself from a certain distance. Life is one long performance. For a short while in high school, I toyed with acting but early on I felt destined to be an artist. There was never really a choice to be made. It is what I am. There was a moment as a young, married mother, when that feeling of detachment, of observing myself from a spot high above from where my actual body was located was so acute it freaked me out. My mind completely separated from my body. It was during a period when the artist part of me was being subsumed by the demands of family life. I tried to explain my dilemma to my husband. He seemed perplexed, suggesting I was making something out of nothing and if I just focused on the job at hand, working with him at M.I.T. and caring for our young daughter, all would be well. He was an indefatigable optimist. But the discontent and feeling of detachment festered. I left him and moved into my converted loft/studio in the old wharf section of Boston five years after that discussion.

Emotional distancing has allowed me to examine the stuff of life, chew on it, digest it and regurgitate it in some other form, just as I'm doing now, in words. Back then, when I literally lived with the art I made, that form was paint on canvas. My experience, my relationships, are stored in my slush pile of inspiration. For others, dwelling on life's most traumatic events and relationships might be debilitating, leading to days, months, even years of grief or regret.

I probably stayed with friends before taking the bus up to Vermont to close on the house I'd bought, thinking it was a perfect location for the two of us. Now it's just me. There was an initial euphoria, an excitement, a sort of unburdening, the freedom of the unknown. I've always loved diving into the unknown. There is great possibility at the beginning of things. It's endings that cause the problems. It's the same with art. The nervous excitement every time I'd stand in front of a blank canvas and the thrill of slashing that white space with a brush load of paint, giving birth to something unrecognizable, but coaxing it into being is still with me but without an adequate studio, it is unrequited.

He elected to stay in Cambridge. I might as well of moved to the arctic circle as far as Ritchie was concerned. After I settled in, I thought he might be tempted to visit. I made it known through mutual friends, that he'd be welcome, but his willingness to simply move on parallelled my own. We were really two of a kind. Once the reality of that became clear, I began a search for a new partner, which led to a string of relationships, some longer and more impactful than others. After Ritchie had his debilitating stroke in 2015, I returned briefly to help clean-up the meager evidence of his life lived on the edge of things. He never was a joiner, always the observer, like me, but unlike me he looked at the world through the cold objectivity of science.

I am a performer in my own life. I need to be the first or the best. I want to hear the applause, get the acceptance, win the award, get the A's. Second place is never good enough. To be ignored is the worst. In this we were opposites. Ritchie avoided competition. He could never do what was necessary to win, especially if he had to conform in any way, particularly when it came to earning a living or having to work for a boss. Authority was anathema to Richie. I took a different route, learning to manipulate any authority figure (usually a man) to get the desired outcome.

I'd documented his stroke and the first year of the aftermath in essays that were published in various literary magazines. In experiencing milestone events, writing is a panacea, providing some clarity. He managed to live, albeit in an incapacitated state, defying all expectations, for ten more years. Today I warily opened that package. I don't know what I expected. A ghost, a vaporous wafting, a sound, perhaps a groan? Inside the standard Express Mail shipping carton sat a sturdy, rectangular, nondescript forest green cardboard box, 8x7x5 inches, weighing about 5 pounds. I gingerly lifted it out reminding myself this was once the body of a man who weighed about 185 pounds in his prime. He was not involved with the usual manly-man sports; he did not have the aggressive drive required to succeed at football, baseball, hockey or basketball. He admitted to having run in tcn Boston Marathons and modestly confessed to have "only completed six."

His legs were powerful. Stocky thighs, muscular calves that came in handy since he walked everywhere and like me, he had no driver's license and also like me, never owned a car. It was one of those quirky things we shared. Those same legs drove him to distraction in the dead of night when his restless-leg syndrome would inevitably prevent sleep. I would sense him getting out of bed, and no matter the season or weather, pulling on his clothes and running shoes to jog up and down the hill in the Fresh Pond Reservation that was just across the street from our Cambridge condo until exhaustion set in and he would stumble home, often sleeping till noon. It was his offbeat circadian rhythm, perhaps exacerbated by a life spent staring at the glow of text on a computer monitor that started long before any of the rest of us even knew what a computer monitor was, that prevented him from ever having a normal-9-to-5 job like most other humans that make a living in our capitalist dominant society, a society that he refused to bend

to even when punishment was meted out for his
noncompliance.

Noncompliance. He was one of those
noncompliant young men who refused to go to the
killing fields of Vietnam. He did a little jail time for
that form of resistance. In his personal
relationships, that might have been construed as
passive aggression. I experienced it as immovable
stubbornness. When I met him, he was still paying
off legal fees he incurred in a case seeking
visitation rights for his only daughter, Cheyenne.
By then Cheyenne was a teenager. The case
happened in the early 1970s. He had refused to
marry the woman involved (she was his first sexual
experience). It was she who introduced him to the
concept of an "alternative lifestyle" living in an
"open relationship" but her definition of freedom
with multiple partners extended only to her. She did
not tolerate any other women in Ritchie's life and
wanted the cover of a bourgeoise lifestyle and the
societal acceptance that marriage offered. Besides,
it's also what her wealthy parents wanted for her.
It's a complicated story as most relationships are
that involve children when the connections between
the parents become frayed beyond repair. Marriage
was no longer in the cards for Ritchie. He'd tasted
freedom and anything less became intolerable.

The woman in question won her case
against him. It caused him deep pain which he
buried but he went on to live without dreaming of
revenge. His former partner never moved on and
spent the rest of her life feeding on the corpse of
their relationship like a zombie. I think she is still
alive, living somewhere in Massachusetts. I wonder

if she knows of his death and if it has supplied her with any relief or sense of closure. I assume she might know as I've been in touch with Cheyenne ever since the stroke when we met for the first time in the ICU at Cambridge City Hospital when it was unclear if her father would survive.

Given his childhood experience with a noncompliant Mormon mom who plowed through a series of four husbands, having children (Ritchie was the oldest) with all but the last one, set Ritchie up for having little respect for the concept of the "nuclear family." His tortured first sexual relationship opened the door to the joys of "free love", a door he walked through and never looked back. Of course, anyone who has tried openly and honestly to live such a life, knows that the notion any love is free is unrealistic. There is always an emotional price to pay for love even if it is given freely with no economic transaction, no legal contract involved. Sex however is a different story. That is widely available both for free and for a price. Emotional attachments not required. For those of us for whom sex has always played an important role in establishing a connection with another human being, we understand the power of this tool when it is treated as a commodity.

I'm trying to decide what I am writing about here. I don't think it's a tribute to this man I knew longer than anyone else, save for my parents and my own daughter. His death had been a longtime coming. He actually died in the ER in 2015 but with heroic efforts on the part of the medical staff at Cambridge City Hospital he survived, but he never again walked the city streets or the path around his beloved Fresh Pond. Maybe I'm attempting to judge what we mean when we talk about "the quality of life". Who gives that life a value? To whom does it matter beyond the mind and body of the person living it? Ritchie was quite brilliant when it came to computer science and more than most of us, he lived inside his head.

I am now at an age when many of the people I have known and perhaps loved, are either dead or close to it. I resist the urge to succumb to the nihilism that seems to have infected the very concept of humanness. Perhaps those letters, HUMAN REMAINS, are prophetic. That is all there is. Ashes to ashes and dust to dust. I'm grounded in the here and now. My parents tried to foist religious training, Christian training, on me while ignoring all such beliefs themselves. I saw and felt the hypocrisy in that. I soon resisted all attempts at church going and so my philistine parents gave up. I think being truly religious demands that you have the capacity to feel and express love, not only for family and friends, but for the world, for life. It requires an energy for living. My parents always appeared to be tired. Never truly happy to simply be alive. They seemed to be on a path that was not determined by them, but they traveled it anyway, without question.

So, what does a person do, a non-religious person, a person bordering on atheism, a person for whom art is their reason to keep on living, what does that person do with human remains? I don't know. For now, that green cardboard box is stowed, out of sight, under my front hall staircase. Maybe that's where it will stay.

Grief Haibun

David Blumenfeld

The thing about grief, they tell me, they say, is not to let it linger, not to wallow in it: purge it. With a therapist, with song, with poetry (write it!), and get on with your life. But how shall I purge my grief for the mother who suckled me, who struggled her whole life with depression, with migraines (shut away in bed in a pitch-black room for days), with shock treatments in the primitive 1940s when it was brutal, when it destroyed her memory, leaving her a half-self, living on the crevice between today and yesterday. Or grief for my father, who knew only sports and the jewelry business, who didn't know how to express love but whose love I knew well, who overate with abandon, smoked three packs a day, and died too young. How shall I purge the grief for my little brother, erased at seven --- polio --- off to camp one bright summer, a smile on his face, in the grave three days later. How can I purge my grief for a wife, belle of my life, eternal blossom, suddenly dead at 49, no warning, just gone, while here I am writing poetry at 88. So, the thing about grief is: you can never purge it. Hold it, embrace it, it's holy pain: ease away from it slowly. The wound heals, the scar remains forever.

Leaves cling to the tree
no matter how hard the storm
some fall far too soon

Libra_Zodiac Highlight

Scales

Heather Bartelt

Balance is my silent song,
a whisper between chaos and calm,
the gentle sway of scales in my hands.

I seek harmony in every breath,
weaving threads of compromise and understanding,
a dance of give and take beneath the surface.

Decisions linger, softly weighted,
not rushing, not rushing—
trusting the pause, the careful weighing of moments.

I am the keeper of equilibrium,
the seeker of fairness in shadows and light,
forever balancing, forever becoming.

Brunch With a Neighbor

Sharisa Aidukaitis

ninety-nine years and ten months
give you the right to make jokes
about how you won't live long
enough to benefit from that home
insurance policy you just renewed,
and that your yellow back lawn will
be someone else's problem soon;

but lacking that same length of life
I doubt I have the right to laugh with
you and I'm struck by the same sense of
impropriety I feel whenever I don't
see you for a few days and I wonder
if you're dead; because we both silently
know that one of these mornings I will

call your landline—the last one in existence
I know of—and you won't answer—
I will be greeted by an electronic echo of
your shaking voice that will no longer
share endless stories of golf and
your nursing career and the million
friends I can't keep straight; but somehow

this truth is only yours to speak and
I can't utter the word death in your presence—
probably because I fear that day when
I will sense the weight of your absence
from down the street, and the three percent
of your life that has overlapped with mine
will be concluded; so I just nod seriously

and say that at least your insurance policy
will give you peace of mind, and you
concede that's true

Fugitive Breath

Sharisa Aidukaitis

I loaded the kids into our aluminum box
of modern peril this weekend to careen
across asphalt for a few hours and

once we finally abandoned our
contraption we summited a vast
boulder with views of dying carbon

fronds and accumulated water droplets
and for a heartbeat we breathed
unfiltered oxygen and were nearly whole

then after we folded our sore limbs
back into the machine, a bird flew
confidently into my fifty mile per

hour rampaging piece of glass
that had no right invading its woods
and as the rearview mirror showed a

suspicious shrinking lump on the road
I cried for the lost fowl whose evolution
didn't prepare it to dodge murderous

jalopies in its peaceful home and I was
still thinking of the creature a few miles
later as I passed a cemetery spilling over

into an elementary school playground

Where Does All the Literacy Go?

William Doreski

As we read without engaging
our bodies we rake up texts
brown as oak leaves in autumn.
No moving our lips, no breath
suspended in stark disbelief,

only the naked sky spreading
rumors of our lack of self
and our refusal to learn more
of the world we'll soon disembody.
You read for the force of prose

breaking on California bluffs.
I read mostly verse that creaks
at the joints and often shatters.
Our piles of books are growing
faster than our bookseller friend

can haul them off to resell.
We can't use the public library
because we'd expose our habits
to people too grim to get jokes
when jokes are badly needed.

The texts eventually will darken
into deep shades of mahogany,
and our reading will cease without
complaint, the lamplight fading
and the political moment past.

You the Utile One

William Doreski

Scrubbing bathroom tiles so hard
they cry aloud, you're pleased
to see yourself in the shine.

The westerly sunlight pours
through the window and bastes you
in a saintly glow. You value

the most ordinary task over
the smug exultations of lawyers
or the afterglow of surgery.

You weed the garden and smile
at the earthworms and crickets,
you clean the cats' litter boxes

with the pride of accomplishment.
I envy your practical stance,
your uninterest in heavy books

except as structural elements
propping up the daily routine.
When you saw reedy young men

lugging electricians' handbooks
to classes on wiring and code
you envied their patient focus

on the years of useful work ahead.
You wish I'd become a plumber
or carpenter. But then I'd fail

to affix you in an aesthetic
simplified and complete enough
to praise your habitual poise.

An Anaphylactic Moment

William Doreski

Ghosts whisper in the waiting room
at midnight. Scripture re-enacts
the losses everyone suffers.
The words are dust on the floor
where the janitorial broom
hardly ever extends itself.
But this hospital space refers
to surgeries, X-rays, healing
gestures of gentle earthen colors.

Hallways converge and funnel
and sort people into patients
and patience, the upright nurses
busy somewhere out of sight
while doctors work with templates.
Emergencies only. The ghosts
reside in a flimsy dimension
to which we'd rather not resort.

The wasp sting that brought us here
has resculpted your face to show
that nature must have its say.
A shot of Benadryl might save you
from your mirror image. Let's hope so.
The late whispers aren't about us,
but they tickle over our skin
like a mist from leaky plumbing
no one will ever bother to fix.

October New Moon Special

The Sun is Hot Today

Junior Baker

I feel the weight of daylight pressing down,
a relentless tide that seeps into my crust,
warmth creeping through every fiber,
a slow surrender to the unyielding blaze.

The air hums heavy, thick with anticipation,
each moment stretching longer than the last,
my edges softening, losing their shape,
as the sun's gaze bears down without mercy.

I am becoming part of this radiant furnace,
a silent witness to my own transformation,
the heat wrapping around me like an old friend,
drawing me closer to an inevitable change.

No escape, just the steady, gentle burn,
a quiet acceptance of the warmth that swallows me,
knowing this too shall pass,
as everything does under the relentless sun.

Variations on a Theme of Spine

Katherine Edgren

I.

Nights it stiffens
        with something other than the forging of
resolve.
As if the vestigial tail, wanting remembering
            whispers:
do not forget you are an animal
        with no more significance
than the trailing ant,
            one day looped to another.

So remember your roots as the stiffness forces you
down
        where
it's easier to crawl on all fours—
        a more natural state.
Aim too high and pain will punish your reach.
        Incompletely evolved as it is
the spine shrieks:
        it's so hard to be upright.

II.

Sometimes for no reason you discover
it unbends, softens

alters from thick, drying stick
to supple branch

gradually turning limber
as if green lumber,

water-soaked willow branches,
or wood-strips curved to form a canoe,

so you bend to pick up your paddle,
step into the boat, and glide through the day.

III.

Her spine served her well for ninety years.
She put her back into climbing hills,
folding donated clothing, rising each morning
with a question on her lips: how can I help?

Yoga, exercise, pills—
she did all anyone could ever do—
but her pages loosened,
slipped to the ground.

Bones crumbled like a dry-stone wall.
Once upright, now bowed,
brought low in the end.
No one could ever claim she had no backbone.

The Glass Fraternity

Joe Del Castillo

Liberty Furnishings offered a full line of styles for apartments and houses, with their core customers being couples starting out. Sales were strong, but returns were a normal business reality. If and when merchandise came back, that's where our crew of three got involved.

At the central warehouse, the furniture, after being unloaded from the trucks, was placed on flat steel carts. Connected to a track embedded in the floor, the goods were hauled in a slow, single-row procession. A low rumble filled the cavern-like warehouse with a muffled hum, like that of a lone, distant airplane, which could be felt all the way to the upstairs records office. Returns veered into our bay for review.

Watching as three carts rolled in was Sandy. Today was his first day in the department. He had transferred from the office. He wore new jeans, a clean shirt, and brown work boots. In time, they would be like mine—old, dirty, and worn. The first cart held a traditional-style desk with curved legs.

"Sandy, help me with this." He and I lifted it onto a long work table, high enough to study it at eye level. Even though his thinning blonde hair and spindly build suggested fragility, he displayed strength in picking up his end easily. "With returns," I instructed, "we determine if the unit is fine as-is or requires some mending. To start an inspection, do a visual of the top and bottom, the sides, and the legs."

"Hey Clay," Rocco, the wrestler-sized refinisher, shouted from his work table. "Tell the new guy that it's like examining a beautiful woman."

The two of us laughed, but Sandy did not. Instead, he glanced at the concrete floor, as if embarrassed. Being his first day, no doubt he felt it was wise to remain quiet and project a serious demeanor.

"With your hands—" I ran mine slowly over the desk— "we feel the wood for nicks and scratches or something worse, like a gash or a crack. Don't go fast, you might cut yourself. Once we fix her, she goes to Rocco."

Wearing denim overalls over a white shirt splattered with shades of brown and maroon colors, Rocco waved a wide stain brush. "I'm the one who finishes the piece and makes it glow, like it's a new morning, as if nothing happened the night before."

The next cart, carrying a pair of small lamp tables, also held a large rectangular glass.

"Glass is different," I said. "It's either perfect or not. Each one is sized to pair with a specific unit, say a table, a desk, or a cabinet shelf. However, occasionally one gets separated from its mate. We'll look and try to match it to its partner, but since we have many styles and shapes, it can become a wild goose chase. We might not even know if the corresponding piece came back. One can waste time searching."

"Like hunting for that perfect woman," Rocco chimed.

This time Sandy laughed a bit. "So Clay, how do we find the right mate? Keep seeking?"

"No. If we don't find her quickly, what we do when the boss, the warehouse manager, isn't around, is take the glass and tap a corner to the floor, just hard enough to clip it. That makes it garbage. Do it gently; you don't want the whole thing to disintegrate on you."

Days later, Sandy stood before me, holding a round glass, the width of a sedan steering wheel.

"What's up?" I asked.

"This top is beautiful," he answered softly. "Look at the beveled edges. They're luminous." As if caressing it, he held it close to his face and slid his hands along the sides. "It's as if the colors of the rainbow were snatched from the sky and are now encircling the glass and making it glow. I've looked for almost an hour, but I didn't find anything that matched."

"Sandy, it's just a piece of glass. You've spent too much time. Give up after fifteen or twenty minutes."

"Clay, are you sure? Can't we put it aside? Maybe the partner will appear. I hate to see it go."

"No, not unless you want to use your company discount to buy it. And what would you do? Lean it against a wall?"

He turned the piece over as if the other side might be different. "If I place it near my bedroom window, it could refract the sunlight and transform my white walls and ceiling into a plethora of colors."

Rocco rose from his table. "Then get yourself a disco ball," he boomed. "Even if it's a Tiffany, it's crap. Get rid of it."

"But I don't think it can be recreated." He wrapped his arms around the piece. "I think it's unique."

Rocco lumbered over to Sandy. "Don't get weird on me." With one hand, he snatched it from him and bumped it against the concrete floor, breaking an end. "Know when to move on."

"Sandy, relax," I called out. "Discarded glass gets recycled."

"It's not the same," he replied, shaking his head and gazing at the floor. "It was one of a kind."

Rocco tapped Sandy's shoulder. "Hey, why did you come here? Why give up the cushy desk job in the office with the nice girls? It must be heavenly with all those women swirling around you, their perfume scenting the air, the pickings you have…"

Sandy leaned toward Rocco's face. "Transferring down here is considered a promotion and got me a pay increase."

His response reminded me that I had once considered the reverse: moving upstairs to a more polished environment. However, going there limited my career growth. Down here, there were opportunities for advancement. Over time, I might even become the manager of the entire facility. That was key if I ever settled down and had a family.

Although quiet and introspective, Sandy proved to be a quick learner, and in about a month, for the most part, he mixed well with us. Like a good newbie, he asked for more work. If overtime was offered, he took it. He preferred to be busy; he'd become unsettled if there wasn't enough work on a given day. While Rocco and I could always shoot the breeze, Sandy would often just listen and drum his fingers, anxious to be doing something with his hands. He'd clean his area, sweep the floor, or reorganize his tools over and over again. At times like this, he became withdrawn. In those silent moods, he might go and take his lunch in an isolated part of the warehouse, a lonely soul almost hidden amid merchandise stacked high on racks. Once I came across Sandy lying on a recliner, staring at a customer order in his hands. I usually didn't pry, but I could tell by its color that it wasn't a return document, therefore not our responsibility.

"Sandy, what are you studying there?" He lowered the sales slip and raised his head slowly, his eyes meeting mine as if he had discovered something profound.

"It's a huge order for Iris Swann," he murmured. "Like she's furnishing a whole house."

"Iris, the customer files clerk? So what? She's taking advantage of the employee discount."

Rubbing his fingers gently across the paper, he said, "Do you know that Iris is also the Greek goddess of the rainbow?"

Huh? Iris was nice, but certainly no goddess. Then again, to each his own. "Sandy, just give me the paperwork. It's not our concern until, if ever, any of it comes back."

As he handed it to me, he looked up at the rafters. "None of it will ever return."

I didn't know how to respond but I started to comprehend that something was eating at him. Frankly, I was never that sensitive to other people's interior emotions—at least that was what my last girlfriend had insisted. For a while, her assertion bothered me, but in time I grew a thicker skin about these things. It helps with the job. As long as my guys don't let personal issues affect their work, I don't ask probing questions. If you need to resolve a problem, take a day off; fix it on your own. It's how I run an efficient department. That discipline makes for good managers.

I mentioned the incident to Rocco, who then said to me, "Clay, I know you're my supervisor, but I strongly suggest you keep an eye on this Sandy dude. You might be missing something."

Often, we grabbed lunch with the other guys in the building. Depending on the weather, we hung outside near the loading dock or inside in the receiving area. Maybe play cards, discuss our favorite teams, or banter about girls, real or imagined. With women, Rocco liked to boast that he met a new girl every weekend. He'd get up, walk back and forth before us, holding his soda cup like a microphone, and act out his latest bad date, turning it into a slapstick comedy. We knew he exaggerated, but he knew how to tell a yarn and kept us in stitches. We all looked forward to the weekly Rocco Show.

A month later, returning from the office, I brought back a flyer. "Hey guys, the boss is having the company cater a lunch for Iris Swann. She's getting married and is moving out of state."

Rocco slapped his forehead in mock sorrow. "Oh no, not Iris! The rainbow goddess never got to know me."

Sandy, a small glass table top in his hands, suddenly trembled and the piece slipped down, struck the floor, and shattered. I had betrayed his privacy by informing Rocco of his rainbow comment.

I glared at Rocco. I wanted to shout *Big mouth! Why did you say that?* Instead, I said, "Was there something between you?"

Sandy walked over to a closet and returned with a broom and dustpan.

"There was nothing," responded Rocco, "but I admit, I did ask her out a few times, but the answer was always a sweet, delicate *no*."

Sandy carried the broken glass to a garbage can near Rocco. He held the dustpan before him. "Rocco, you never had a prayer with her. She's had a ring on for months."

Rocco shrugged his shoulders. "I never noticed. It doesn't matter. End of story."

Sandy dumped the trash into the receptacle.

"Anyway," I said, trying to defuse the tension. "On Friday, let's have some fun. Let's party, stuff ourselves, and bid farewell."

"I'll pass," Sandy said.

"Really? We never miss an event when the boss is hosting. And you could help the girls to get to know me better."

"Clay," he chuckled, "you'll do fine without me."

Rocco slapped his knee. "And another one bites the dust."

On Friday, I called Sandy on his phone. "Hey man, it's a good party. We're having a great time. Some really good food, too. Your old office mates miss you. Why not come up?"

"Thanks, but no. How are you guys doing with the girls?"

"We're doing great. I think they find us fascinating. Except for Iris. She's upset that you didn't show up."

"Wish her well for me."

Before I could react, Sandy turned off his cell. I thought of him sitting alone in the warehouse, possibly in one of his moods. I then felt the drone rumble of the conveyor lines, which had been shut off, start up. Something wasn't right. You don't run the units without other staff present. I signaled Rocco to follow me as I hurried out of the office and down the stairs. I made my way through the long aisles, past the receiving department, and heard a crash. Reaching my section, I found Sandy crouched by a mound of broken glass, staring at the smashed pieces. The high shop lights, shining down onto the fragments, created a swirl of prismatic colors that reflected across his face. He slid his hands back and forth, skimming the top layers of the shards. That his fingers were scratched and cut did not concern him.

Additional glass tops and shelves were lined up in the carts. I realized that he had intended to destroy those too if I hadn't come.

Rocco arrived. "What's going on?"

"I'm not sure." Taking Sandy's arm, I pulled him up, and he followed, like a sleepwalker, away from the rubble to a nearby chair.

"Sit down," I directed. "Take a deep breath. Now, tell me, what's happened?"

Rocco grabbed a broom and began to sweep up the debris.

"How was the party?" Sandy asked, the look in his eyes hollow. "How was Iris?"

I knelt alongside him. "She appreciated everyone's good wishes," I said, "but Iris was very hurt that you didn't go up to see her. She said that she considered you a close friend and that she had been honest with you. Saying goodbye was the least you could have done."

Staring at his pants, he smeared blood onto them. "It was something I could not bear to do."

With my handkerchief, I wiped one of his hands.

"I see," I said. "I'm sorry, but if you follow our lead and hang tough, over time, you'll get over her."

"He's right," Rocco said. Using the broom as a crutch, he got down on the other side. "But it depends how you bear it," he continued. "You have three choices. You can remain as soft as sand or thicken into clay, or better yet, become as hard as rock."

Three Dreams Remain

Kenneth Boyd

Part One: Creatures Dream

Healing our coin-operated sorrow
Sorrow replayed when the lands are barren
Barren like waters where whales burst and pose
Breach in the sky where birds could know freedom
Freedom we hold tight when the seas are dry
Dry seabed that appears to be sleeping
Sleeping in nature is a shifting state
State of a deciduous vigil
Vigil for the unappreciated
Unappreciated Dreams will vanish

Part Two: Birds Dream

Unappreciated dreams will vanish
Earth's polluted air and dirty water
Water from a comorbid vanity
Vanity of a bird that flies above
Above where they pose in the lift of winds
Winds where they wait like drafting gliders
Gliders, silent, in search of a small slice crack
Crack of light splicing the verve to escape
Escape the comorbidity of earth
Earth, our earth, too long you rest unaware

Part Three: Mothers Dream

Earth, our earth, too long you rest unaware
Unaware of our trespass on God's forms
Forms and images seen as gifted jewels
Jewels to Titans, singing of the elements
Elements conspiring at rest and run
Run with Terra, the goddess and mother
Mother Terra, sing for fruit and flowers
Flowers to inspire oratorios
Oratorios sung in shrines of trees
Trees aspiring to immortality

November Full Moon Special

Fading Hour

Heather Bartelt

The clock's slow crawl, a whispered breath,
A hollow ache that lingers, cold and deep.
Fingers clutch the fading light of day,
While silent fears inside me creep.

A weight unspoken presses near,
Unseen, yet heavy on my chest.
The quiet hum of time's advance,
A relentless march I can't arrest.

Fingers tremble, breath grows thin,
A fragile shell in twilight's grip.
The final hush begins to swell,
As moments slip through grasping slip.

In this faint dusk, I stand alone,
Uncertain of what waits beyond,
A silent, creeping, endless ache,
Beneath the stillness, unspoken, gone.

NOTHING MORE DELIVERED

John Grey

Uncle Bert
sat on his porch,
large and gray-skinned
as a hippo.

Service in Korea,
ten years owning his own garage
followed by forty working in someone else's,
a quarter-century marriage,
three kids, a lifelong nicotine habit,
two bouts with cancer,
were all writ large
in that imposing but decaying body.

No longer built for flexibility,
he set his lowering sights
on comfort:
a rocking chair,
a convenient place
to both see life pass by
and make it to the bathroom on time.

That was where the mailman found him.
His "Hello, Mr. Jenkins,
just bills today, I'm afraid"
was answered by
that most resolute of silences.

Korea, garage,
wife, kids, cigarettes, disease –
death stopped anything more from happening.

JIGSAW PUZZLE

John Grey

The puzzle is the lone survivor of so many.
For some reason, it was saved,
if being stashed away in an attic trunk
        is rescue.

He's back from the war,
from one pitiful truth to another,
scouring through out-of-vogue moments
        from the past.

There it is, beneath musty letters
and a decaying wedding dress,
a sun-ripened landscape never to be
        put together again.

He can remember being consumed
by the picture on the box,
a Hudson valley scene, a symmetrical
        green and blue,

and a castle on a hill, sublime, romantic,
at an age when he was fearful of those words
as spoken but not when patched together.
        by hand.

And here it is,
lonelier even than his life,
passed down to a non-existent generation,
        waters stagnant,

green hills damp with brown,
castle shuttered, no longer to be solved
but to be pitied, one thousand pieces
        plus one.

An Event at City Hospital

Joe Del Castillo

Two City Hospital orderlies maneuvered the gurney from the corridor into the room. The doctor followed in. "Easy now," he said. Gently, they lifted the invalid onto the bed. With a wave, he dismissed the attendants.

The young physician pulled over a chair, sat down, and spoke softly. "Sir, can you hear me?"

The middle-aged man opened his eyes and raised a hand. "Yes…even though I feel like I'm in the Twilight Zone."

"That's expected, but be assured, you're improving. However, we had to place you in a shared room because of the overcrowding. Leaving you in a corridor was not an option for our governor."

"I don't have my own room?"

The doctor patted the man's hand. "Don't worry, you have the best care."

It had only been a couple of hours, but the governor recalled bits and pieces of what happened: a gunshot, people screaming, his guards pushing him to the ground, an ambulance siren. In the emergency room, lying on his back with the ceiling lights blinding him, nurses and doctors, all in PPE gowns and masks, scrambled and shouted over him. The governor, himself a film buff, was reminded of movies in which the populace flees the zombies.

"As I was saying," continued the doctor, "it's a shared room." He pointed to a curtain that hung between the beds. "Instead of the usual fabric, we're using plastic to reduce the possibility of transference."

The other side was dark, but one could make out a white sheet covering a person.

"He was struck by the bullet that went through you."

"Oh no." The governor tried to rise. "Let me see him."

"Sir," the doctor said, placing his hand on the man's chest. "Please remain as still as possible. The bullet missed your heart by millimeters; I need a day to confirm that all is good. Tomorrow, we'll get you walking, and you should be out a day later. You were lucky in how you were spared."

"Then I'll talk with him."

"You can't. He's comatose. The reality is that he won't make it. It's a matter of hours, if not minutes." The doctor checked the wall clock: 2:05 PM.

"There's nothing you can do?" asked the governor.

"There's nothing I can do."

"You're very matter-of-fact about this."

"It is what it is." The physician showed a smile of reassurance. "However, for you, it's a second chance, but I need you to stay in bed. I want to make sure everything is fine so you can return to your duties."

The governor felt remorseful. Someone had tried to kill him as he campaigned for re-election, and now, a few feet over, was a total stranger, about to die for him. "What did he do?"

"Oh, I don't know. With all that's going on, there's little time to get into someone's background." The doctor leaned closer and spoke gently. "I'm going to speak out of line. I hope you agree that this incident, in its random way, can be fortuitous."

"Incident? You call being shot an 'incident'? Such a trivial word! Someone tried to assassinate me! This is an *event*, not an incident."

The doctor sat back. "You're right, it's an event, a major event. And there are reporters downstairs clamoring to see you. Due to the virus, we can keep them out."

"I understand." The governor seemed satisfied. "But it's good that they're out there."

"Sir, it's not my business to give opinions unless they are medical. But what I'm going to say is related to your health.

"I disagree with many of the things you stand for. I won't get into specifics, but consider this: in essence, you've been reborn. This can be an opportunity for you to redirect your energies in a positive manner. Instead of anger, embrace humility. Rather than tear down, build up. Instead of dividing—" the doctor clasped his hands "—bring together. Don't waste this chance."

"Are you getting spiritual with me?"

"Oh no, not me," the doctor laughed. "I'm strictly science, but think about what I said. And please try to sleep and stay as still as possible." He stood. "I've assigned our best RN to keep tabs on you." He shook the man's hand and departed the room.

Whenever the governor heard suggestions as the doctor gave, he usually lashed out, becoming loud, calling the others names, and belittling their intelligence and ethnic origins. But now, he felt conflicted. The physician's points were valid, but if he took the advice, he would have to explain his transformation to his legion of admirers. They supported him exactly for what the doctor criticized him for. If he reversed his position, his followers no doubt would desert him and find a new leader. If he did a 180 on his promises, he needed to come up with excuses. He would not be able to blame others as he usually did. No, a complete about-face of policies would be political suicide.

His guard detail, a man and a woman, both wearing masks, stood outside the door. They knew their governor. Sooner or later, he would castigate them for the security lapse. The RN approached them, pushing the monitor unit. The female guard did a quick search while the other inspected the machine.

"Hello, sir. I'm here to take your vitals."

Despite the gown, mask, and gloves she wore, her body took his mind off his ambivalence. He recalled porn movies with nurses. Even better, he remembered compliant women from over the years.

She placed her stethoscope on his chest. When she finished listening and began to step back, the governor took hold of the round piece. "After you finish, may I take *your* vitals?"

"Not a good idea," she laughed. She was used to handling these situations. "Your wife is due any moment from her trip. I'm sure she won't approve. I hear she's a saint—" Realizing she was getting personal, she stopped and, instead, said. "Besides, in a tussle, I could do bad things to you, like accidentally remove the IV in your arm or knock your bedpan out."

"Won't you reconsider? The guards know the drill."

The nurse stood up straight. "I'm married, I keep my commitments."

He changed tactics. "Nurse, do you know anything about the gentleman over there?"

"I heard that he managed a soup kitchen."

The governor contemplated the different histories between them. He, born rich and well connected, and the soup kitchen guy, probably a poor slob who spent his time with the even less fortunate. Heck, they both did what they thought was best for the common good.

"Nurse, if you won't take this opportunity with me, could you at least open the drapes and let in some light?"

"That I can do." Pulling them back, the view revealed a multi-story apartment building across the avenue. Hanging from the third-floor balcony was a large banner with the painted words, "Don't Let This Incident Change Your Goals." A small group waved from behind the sign.

Incident? The governor scowled and made a fist.

"On second thought, they need to be shut."

"Those are my people! I can acknowledge them."

"Sorry, for your security, they have to be closed. It's ironic. According to the cops, the gunman has confessed to being one of your supporters who felt you were soft on your issues."

"What do you mean?"

The RN read the monitor on the machines. "Your signs are improving. Try to relax and sleep."

"Nurse, I asked you a question. What do you mean, ironic?"

She stopped entering the data. She wanted to berate this man, but understood she should not, but what the hell. Lately, the hospital felt like the end of the world.

"Somehow—" the nurse placed her hands on her hips. "—one can summarize your policies into equations like, 'More guns equal less violence. Vaccines spread disease. Do you know how crazy that is?"

"That's enough!" He slammed his hand down on the bed.

"Sir, don't strain yourself." As much as she despised him, the last thing she wanted was to make him worse. "I'm sorry. I'll shut up." Besides, the sooner he left, the quicker another patient could get a bed.

He reached out to her. "Come, take my hand. Sit on the bed and be nice to me, and I'll pardon your comments."

"Sir, there's too much going on. Try prayer; they can prevent the rust that is building in your soul."

"Oh, you're the spiritual one."

"I need to check your roommate and get to the other cases." The nurse rolled the machine to the other side. She took the man's wrist and counted to 60. She placed the stethoscope on the chest. She checked the pupils and, with tears in her eyes, whispered, "This man has passed." The RN made the sign of the cross and pulled the sheet over the man's face. She looked at the clock: 2:25 PM. Quickly, she pushed the unit and passed the governor.

"I heard you say he's dead."

"Yes, but a doctor has to make it official." She hurried out of the room.

He tried to look through the plastic barrier, but it was too thick, the section too dark, to make out any details except for the outline of the body and the white sheet over it. Whoever he was, the governor would pay for the funeral and exalt the victim as a martyr. He would use the innocent bystander's death to double down on his agenda.

He was tired and knew he should try to sleep. The governor shifted slowly and tried to nod off, but could not. He found himself staring at the dead man. As if his head was frozen in position and his eyes would not shut. He felt his throat dry up. With a rasp, he called for one of his guards, and the man stepped in.

"Chuck, the guy in the bed has died. See what's taking so long for the doctor to get back so he can be removed. It's creeping me out." *Of course, as soon as they remove him, they'll bring another patient in.*

"Sir," he answered. "The staff is overloaded. They're trying to move other victims out, but they're debating where to take the bodies."

Feeling the floor rumble as the machines and gurneys were wheeled along the corridor, the governor peered at the curtain. Against his will, his thoughts began to flood with scenes of old horror movies where the dead come to life. His mind saw hands break out of graves, bodies emerge and rise, and, like wide-eyed sleepwalkers with arms extended, stalk the living. What was happening?

"Chuck, no excuses, do something about it!"

The guard ran out.

The governor stared at the clock. Ten minutes went by, fifteen, and still no one came in.

A man's voice, high-pitched but weak, as if something was caught in his throat, spoke from the other side. "The bullet was meant for you, not for me."

"Huh?" The startled governor focused on the curtain separating him from the dead man.

"The bullet—it was meant for you. But it got me."

The governor tried to move but could not. "Um…yes, I know. But it's not my fault. The bullet almost got me. It could have been me. I got lucky."

"I sure wasn't," said the voice, taking deep breaths and becoming clearer. "And now you're going to pay for my funeral and make me some kind of martyr? My death is supposed to get you re-elected?"

"How can you know my thoughts?" He gripped the call button, pressing it repeatedly. "How can you know that?"

The body did not move. However, it continued to speak. "Governor, I'm no angel, but compared to you, I was a Boy Scout."

The governor shook his head. "Stop it. This can't be." With the strange voice and memories of horror films overtaking him, he reached for the remote and clicked on the TV. It was the news, and it was about him. Turning the volume up, he watched crowds scream at each other and shake signs with opposing messages.

"I forgive you," said the man, his voice rising.

"Forgive what?"

"I forgive you for the lies you have spread throughout your life."

"Chuck, get in here!" The governor tried to holler, but his voice faltered, lowering to a whisper.

No answer. The governor kept pressing the call button. He heard people run in the halls, shout, and call for help.

The voice changed and became a woman's. "I forgive you for all your philandering."

My god! It's my wife. Starting to pant, his head snapped back and forth: she was not there.

The voice became masculine again, this time sounding much older, like a man critically ill, barely able to get a word out. "Son…forgive me for instilling in you…all the wrong values. I'm so ashamed for instructing you…on how to cheat your way through life. But you were smart. You should have known better."

Through the curtain, he saw the body, a shadowy silhouette, rise. A hand lifted the curtain halfway, enough for legs to come over and hang over the side of the bed. The governor saw the white hem of the gown fall between the knees and ankles. The other hand reached to the side of the curtain and began to pull it back.

The governor's body jerked. He trembled, he shook, and, trying to make himself sit up and get out, he instead heaved over, rolling off and crashing onto the floor, dragging the IV stand down onto him.

The nurse and doctor rushed in. The physician dropped down and began striking the man's chest. "Damn it! I told him to stay put. What the hell possessed him?"

"The TV's on," said the RN, "and the news is all about him. Maybe it agitated him."

"He started talking and shouting questions," announced the voice, now younger and resonant. The medic's head popped up. "He was out of control. Suddenly, I heard a crash."

The doctor rose, and the RN knelt, their eyes widening upon seeing the man in the white hospital gown, sitting up.

The doctor looked down. "Didn't you say he was—"

"I swear, there was no pulse, no signs," she shouted. "I don't understand!"

The physician whispered. "My God, how do you feel?"

"At first, like I was on death's door," he answered. He raised his arms, the sleeves of the gown pulled up, and laughed. "But now, I feel vigorous. I feel reborn."

The nurse took the governor's hand and clasped it in hers. Closing her eyes, she held it for a moment and then let go. She made the sign of the cross and, tears in her eyes, gazed at the doctor.

He glanced at the clock. "Time of death, 3 PM. Inform the staff that we have two free beds."

———

Scorpio Zodiac Highlight

To Be Yours

Zayn Dorsey

In the quiet hours, I linger at the edge
of your shadow, a breath away from the touch
that never comes yet always lingers.

There's a flicker—something fierce, dormant,
waiting beneath the surface—
a fire that whispers your name in silence,
a hunger that hums beneath my skin.

Your eyes hold secrets I long to unravel,
a promise of chaos and calm entwined,
drawing me closer with unspoken gravity.

I am the storm that brews behind your gaze,
the quiet pulse beneath your skin—
a desire that refuses to be named,
but aches to be felt,
to be consumed,
to be yours.

Old Man Winter Comes to Call

Daneen Fox

Decaying leaves lay like rags
on the tree beyond the window threads.
Creaking in the wooden rocker, the woman
sighs to the tune of the fire's hums.
Her practiced hand flits
across the linen snow

in her lap. The sky cries more snow
that makes the curtain-rags
whine. Skeletal mice flit
from their holes to the threads
of the fire warmed rug and hum
to the rhythm of the woman.

The fire tells the woman
it is losing to the growing snow.
Two more logs create a satisfied hum.
She draws her rags
closer and paints in faded threads,
watching the needle flit

as the leaves flit,
leaving behind the touch of a woman.
The barren tree threads
its arthritic fingers in the snow
that falls in rags
and in the intimacy, hums.

The skeletal mice hum

in slumber and flit
their tails across the worn rags
at the feet of the woman.
Her carefully pinned head of snow
escapes in silken threads.

The unforgiving window threads
dance as the wind hums.
Forgetting the linen snow
in her lap, she flits
with the grace of an aged woman
to tighten the billowing rags.

The soft threads of her hair flit
in the wind that hums along with the woman
as she watches the snow fall in rags.

Helping Myra

Larry Pike

My book group met this afternoon. The women in the group are my best friends. We were a group long before Oprah or Reese or even Jenna said reading was a good idea. Some Wednesdays, especially thick summer days like this one, we gather at Maggie's cottage on Lake Lee. If the group's not too large or the weather too bad, we'll take Maggie and Simon's pontoon boat out for the afternoon. Other days, we may lunch at a new restaurant, like the Bohemian-revival café on 13th or the faux adobe Mexican cantina near where the College Glen Mall used to be. The old mall space now houses a small business development center, or something, run by our local university, which has propped up the area. Most often, though, we'll meet at Rachel's where we'll lounge on the deck that flows around a huge, spreading tree.

I don't know trees. Rachel does. At a party once, Rachel overheard me telling someone about the tree. I called it a sugar maple. Rachel laughed loudly enough that I was embarrassed, and she never did tell me what it is. A live oak, maybe. The deck is in full shade by early afternoon. You can chat comfortably there for hours, and we usually do.

I always read our assigned stories, in case we talk about them.

We didn't discuss a story today. We met at the landfill today. Instead of sipping one of Phyllis's superb margaritas, as I'd have preferred, reclining in one of Rachel's cushy floral-print chaises with

the molded-in drink holders, I perched on the
tailgate of a big, dirty Ford pickup. I've seen men in
commercials sit like that. They always look at ease,
which says something about truth-in-advertising or
the indulgent relationship men have with the world
because I definitely did not enjoy it. The truck was
backed right up to the edge of the landfill's pit, and
the bed was piled way beyond the recommended
payload limit.

This was Myra's fault. She presumed, as is her
way, that the group would love to help her unload
the truck. She didn't clear this with anyone. Myra
said, after parking the borrowed truck in Rachel's
driveway, "It'll be an adventure." It wasn't. I'd
already claimed my favorite chaise on Rachel's
deck. Rather than relaxing in the company of my
friends, I got hotter and sweatier and even thirstier
for my margarita, which if I had had right then I
would have gulped down even before licking all the
glorious coarse salt from the rim of the glass.
Instead of the tequila, I gulped in the stench of the
whole town's rotting garbage being folded under by
a bulldozer in the pit. I plan to recycle more.

"Don't talk about the story today, I didn't read
it," Myra told us at Rachel's. Myra never reads the
stories. She said this with the toss of her head that
swings her dark hair over her shoulder. The hair
doesn't stay back, of course. I want her to tie it
back, put a barrette in it, cut it, something, just stop
the head-bobbing. "Help me haul this debris to the
dump." Myra takes extension classes across town at
State, and regularly uses words like *debris*. She says
utilizes, too, instead of *uses*.

What Myra wanted our help with represented
the physical remains of her marriage to Rich. Their

split was not friendly, and divorcing Rich, a pharmacist who owns several neighborhood drugstores, and who had the habit of grinding his mortar, shall I say, in any random, available pestle, had been Myra's virtual job for over a year. She put in a lot of overtime on the project. Myra rarely started or joined a conversation without steering the talk to her agonizing marital experience. It's a wonder she hadn't created her own website, a broken-home page. Myra got so bad she couldn't have gotten on a PTA committee. We almost excluded her from the book group because of her behavior, but Maggie prevailed on us to indulge Myra. "After all," Maggie reasoned, "Rich *is* an s.o.b." Because of the boat, we defer to Maggie a lot.

*

Phyl and C.J. rode to the dump in the truck with Myra. Rachel and I, along with Denise and Denise's terrier, Emily, followed in Rachel's car, which was a good thing. Emily is cute enough, for a dog, but I wouldn't have let her in my car, so if I'd had to drive, Denise probably wouldn't have gone with us. Wherever Denise goes, Emily has to go, too. There was no good reason for Denise to miss the fun, not if the rest of us had to endure it. As it was, we lost Maggie, who said she had a meeting to attend and couldn't stay too long anyway. Everyone but Myra knew better. Despite her encouragement to us, Maggie isn't that tolerant with Myra.

The clerk at the landfill's scale station, a big guy with wraparound sunglasses, weighed Myra's truck. We could see his face, shiny in the heat,

147

through the window as he listened to Myra. She pointed back to us, and the man looked in our direction and nodded. When Myra pulled off the scale, he waved us through.

Emily, at least, was excited. She stood with her paws on the back of the seat, looking out the rear window, next to Denise. She panted noisily, and registered one-note barks as the occasional gravel ricocheted off the underside of the car. I wouldn't have figured driving a stick-shift for one of Myra's skills, but she handled the truck well. It didn't lurch when she worked the clutch. She seemed familiar with the dirt track, and disappeared over a hill. When we topped the rise, I saw the pit ahead. There were a few other pickups and a city garbage truck emptying their loads. Myra wheeled around last along the row past the city truck, and backed up to the pit. Rachel parked grille-to-grille with Myra's truck.

The five of us and Emily stood around the pickup, waiting to hear Myra's plan. We expected too much. Myra simply lowered the tailgate and said, "Let's get it out of here."

It was like the burial at sea of one's enemy, though lacking the essential respectful, if grudging, dignity, and certainly lacking water. Myra was saying good-bye to about a ton of small items and some good furniture. I couldn't picture what would be left in her house. Some pieces required two or three of us to drag them out of the bed and shove them into the pit. With what Myra could manage by herself she said a few bitter, precise words about whatever atrocity of Rich's the item brought to mind, then dropped it into the pit. "Rich utilized this Makita cordless drill," she said one time, holding the tool like a large caliber pistol, "to put a very smooth half-inch hole in the center of my grandmother's cherry dining table." Stuff like that. I understood Myra's anger, but the drill looked brand new. I almost asked if she would mind if we took home some of the things, like the circular saw that preceded the drill into the pit. My husband, Steve, mentioned something last week about needing a circular saw.

We worked hard clearing out the truck. The dust clung to our slick arms and legs, not heavy enough to be a mud pack exactly, but pretty slimy. Emily was going to need a bath. Also, a blister was raised on my left heel by the strap of my sandal. You can't work at the landfill in sandals. Another city garbage truck had rolled up to the pit next to us. All the men on the city trucks, I noticed, wore heavy, sturdy shoes. Professionals obviously.

The bed to Myra's truck was half-empty when we got to the sofa. Myra couldn't jerk this heavy item out alone, so Rachel and C.J. climbed up to help. The high-backed sofa was very formal, upholstered in a fancy striped fabric, all plum and grape and creamy butter. An object for a big living room, it could seat four adults, and showed limited wear, a description that would not apply by the time it was removed from the truck. One of its legs had wedged into a hole in the bed's floor. Myra, Rachel and C.J. pushed and pulled, but their efforts lacked leverage. They didn't dislodge the leg, but did loosen one of the arms from the back of the couch. As they struggled I saw the men of the crew of the garbage truck next to us watching them, laughing among themselves. All except one, a pleasant looking guy with thick, graying hair and intelligent eyes. By that I mean compared to his co-workers'.

"I hate this sofa," Myra said, putting her hip smartly to the loose arm one last, dejected time.

C.J., barely a size 5, a real lightweight with close-cropped auburn hair, flopped onto the couch. "Can we go back to throwing out small tools?" she asked.

"We'll get it, if you'll get up, C.J.," said Rachel. She was practical and didn't hesitate to take charge. She touched Myra's shoulder, a tender gesture for Rachel, whose usual style of support was a terse *Get a life*, but Myra waved her away.

"No, that's not it. We'll get it, it's just stuck. I just *hate* this sofa. I think Derrick was conceived right here, maybe Julie too." Myra rubbed a hand across a spot along the top of the high back. "Derrick's voice is changing. Sometimes I hear him talking in another room, and I don't recognize him. So many men, and I had to pick Rich."

Rachel and C.J., Phyl and I exchanged looks as Myra smoothed her hands down her hips.

"You know, he liked it from behind," Myra continued. "This couch was just the right height to bend me over. Whenever the urge struck him, middle of the day, UPS guy at the door, whatever. Foreplay was me saying, 'No, Rich, not here, not right now.' Very romantic." C.J. quickly jumped up.

Rachel said, "That's disgusting, Myra."

"You think so? At least he wasn't breathing in my face."

The pause that followed was broken finally by Denise who had been up on her toes, leaning into the bed, busily moving things around. She pulled out a photo album and held it out to Myra. Denise's white shorts were reddish-orange across the front where she'd been against the truck. "You can't throw this away. It's got pictures of the kids."

Myra didn't reach for the album. "Rich, too. He could've taken them."

Denise kept her eyes on Myra, but handed the album over to Phyllis, who was standing by me. "Look," Denise said.

Phyllis opened the album. She tilted it so I could see it, too. Under the protective sheets were prints made on a home printer, some trimmed from plain copy paper, that could've belonged to any family. Myra, still heavy from the pregnancy, standing by the van, holding a baby—Julie, not Derrick, because the van arrived shortly before Julie did. The kids playing at the beach, covering Rich with sand. Julie in her tee-ball uniform. Derrick as one of the wise men in a church pageant, his crown too big, slid down to his eyebrows. The backs of a bunch of kids in pointed birthday hats huddled around the kitchen table.

Another photo, a recent one, was loose between a couple of pages. It was of Rich and the children, with Mickey Mouse in the background, taken over this past spring break at Disney World. Rich had flown the kids down, Myra said, as a reminder that he could do it and she couldn't. Evidently, he asked someone to shoot their picture with his phone. Rich is smiling, but it's a hard, thin smile; it looked to me like he was having to work at enjoying the day, and his grip on the kids might have been a bit tight. Julie has dipped her shoulder a little, like she's trying to slip out of Rich's grasp, and Derrick is not looking at the lens. Clearly, they were not in the Magic Kingdom.

"Rich is good looking," said Phyllis without thinking, as she tends to do, more or less to me, but Myra heard her, too.

"For a Neanderthal."

C.J., still up in the truck, said, "It's okay to hate him, but Rich is still their father." I figured C.J. knew what she was talking about. She divorced Bobby about three years ago. If you didn't know C.J. had three children, you'd never know she'd been married. I'm happily married, I think, but maybe I shouldn't be, married I mean, judging by C.J.

Phyllis closed the album. "Even if you don't want them, Derrick and Julie will someday," she said to Myra.

"Tell me about hating him again," Myra said. "I like that part."

Phyllis waited until Myra wasn't looking, then tossed the photo album into the cab of the truck.

*

We hadn't made headway on the sofa, or anything else. The heat had sapped the little organization we'd had. We stood around the truck not talking, pretty mad at Rich—and Myra—for ruining our afternoon.

The city truck parked next to us cranked up, and belched a heavy cloud of smoke. I don't see how the workers could stand riding in it all day with that noise. As it pulled away, a man on the crew waved to the driver. He was the one who hadn't laughed at us earlier. He walked toward us. Myra saw him, and whispered to Rachel, "He's kind of cute."

Rachel rolled her eyes.

"May I help you ladies?" the man asked as he neared.

I noticed his syntax right away, *may* instead of *can*.

Rachel preempted Myra. "You missed your ride."

He looked past us at the departing truck, and smiled agreeably. "It's not that far back out."

I guessed him to be late-forties, maybe a little older. He was nice looking. You could take him home to meet your folks without getting the third degree. He looked good in the city's sanitation department uniform, light green shirt, dark green pants. His well-worn work boots looked comfortable and reminded me of my blistered foot.

"I'm Alex," he said, thumbing the patch on his shirt. "Need some help?" We nodded and he hopped into the truck's bed.

C.J. said, "The couch is stuck."

He inspected it. "Why're you throwing this out? Looks okay."

Myra said, pointing, "It has a broken arm."

Alex reached over and moved the arm several times. "This could probably be fixed."

"Probably."

"But you don't want to."

"No."

"She's just divorced. It belonged to her and Rich," Phyllis blurted. Myra turned and shot her a vicious look. I cringed, moving out of the line of fire.

Alex didn't react. "It won't take much to move this." He positioned himself at the corner of the sofa. He used good lifting technique, his legs doing the work instead of his back. On his third try, the jammed leg popped free with the painful sound of groaning metal. Alex rotated the sofa enough to put the leg down on a solid spot. He stood up and wiped his hands. "There."

With little subtlety, Myra moved up to the side of the truck next to where Alex stood in the bed, closer than I thought necessary, to say thanks. She pulled coyly at the loose fuchsia pullover that matched the swooping stripe on her black cyclist's shorts. Myra wears a lot of athleisure styles, brands like lululemon and Athleta. Vuori. She's a regular poster child for high-end merchandisers. The shorts were a padded kind, a style she favors because she has no butt, a fashion decision I will never need to make. Three or four years ago, Rich wanted her to have augmentation, but the process scared her. *What if it turns out lumpy?* she wailed to us at the time. *Compared to what you've got now, honey,* we told her, *anything would be lumpy.* She decided not to risk it.

She was performing her hair-swinging trick.

"You're welcome," Alex said. He didn't seem interested in the hair. Myra noticed this, too. She flipped it again and then brushed it back slowly with her hand twice. Her eagerness festered.

She tried another approach. "Would you like some of these things before we throw them out?" I knew I should have asked about the circular saw. Myra's offer to rummage through the pile did not extend to her general helper population.

"I'll take a look."

Alex worked around the bed of the truck, squatting. He picked out a couple of small items, an electric shaver and some kind of big wrench, and set them aside. He held up a small open jewelry box. He had large hands. "These earrings, too?"

"Too what?"

"Throwing them away?"

"Everything."

"Nice pearls. Not costume."

Myra pretended to look carefully at them. "Oh, those?" she said with a quick laugh. "Those are from my cra with Alan. He was such a good earring buyer. How do you know they're real?"

"Worked in a jewelry store once. Nice atmosphere, crummy hours. Thought your friend said your ex's name was Rich?"

"Alan was before."

"Another ex?"

Myra flinched. "No."

That would depend on how you looked at things. Alan was before Myra married Rich. He was *during*, too. I'm the only one who knows this. I was at Myra's one day a couple of years ago, before Myra pulled the plug on her marriage, helping with some project or another. We'd been drinking a nice, fruity white most of the afternoon, which had slowed our progress, though Myra didn't care. Halfway through a second bottle she let it slip about hooking up with Alan again. She panicked and swore me to secrecy.

Which I have maintained. I've never told anyone, especially not Maggie, who would not appreciate Myra's Pitiful Pearl act while carrying on just like Rich. Never even mentioned it again to Myra. Though to be perfectly honest, I'm a little conflicted. Sometimes when she goes on about what an asshole Rich was, not keeping it in his pants and all, I want to remind her that Rich's khakis weren't the only ones not always pulled up. You know, live and learn? But I hold my tongue. Despite all her classes at State, Myra isn't into self-reflection.

Alex said, "If he bought such good jewelry, should've married him."

"Maybe."

Alex shrugged. "You don't want them, I'll take them, too. My wife will like them."

"Your wife?" Myra asked. Everybody registered the disappointment in her voice.

"She'd wear something thrown out in a divorce?" Denise asked.

"Not her divorce. Could've bought them at a yard sale or an antique shop. No different."

"Where will you tell her you got them?" C.J. asked.

"Here. Thought that counts."

C. J. snorted. No one else could think of a reply. Myra didn't move. In the pit below us, the bulldozer churned.

"Anything else like these?" Alex finally asked. Absently, Myra shook her head. He pocketed the little box. "Let me pitch this in the pit, then, and we can all go home."

Alex cleared the bed quickly. If Myra had hired him to haul this load for her in the first place, the job would have been done much faster—and we wouldn't have been involved in it. We'd never have left Rachel's, and I'd have enjoyed my margarita. Alex moved with the economy of one used to a job. His shirt stuck to his back, and dark ovals of sweat stained his underarms, but he did look good. I caught Myra watching his arms. They were tanned and firm. I noticed them, too. A long scratch was healing on one forearm, a pink line where the scab had been. His hands were dirty, of course, but looked like he took good care of them. His nails were trimmed.

We thanked Alex for his help. He asked if we'd give him a ride out to the scale house. Myra didn't answer, just opened the door and got behind the wheel of the truck. Rachel looked at her for a moment, then said to Alex, "Hop in the back of the truck, if that's okay. All our passenger room is taken."

The rest of us piled in the vehicles we came in. Emily, her tongue out, curled up on the seat beside Denise.

The last we saw of Alex before he vanished was the little salute he gave us. Myra was not as smooth with the clutch as before, and he bounced through each shift of the gears. Rachel hung back, trying to keep from running us off the road in the dust that swirled up from Myra's truck.

November New Moon Special

Nocturnal Nature

N. Mohanarangam

Pensively promenaded I, as impetuous as a poet
To accumulate few jocund inkling on dusk

For sure, not as a bard
But, as a novice to nature

Stalked I, bare-footed anigh lake
Jabbed some spines beneath my foot

Yon reconnoitred I, do any luminous light
clandestined in water?
Else, any celestial gem floats in lake?

Nay! it's the waxing moon in the sky
That seemed to tread on water.

Paddled I into the lake
To grab some pallied lilies

Hardly perceived I any bloomed one!
Had the lilies been sailed under false color by
moon?

I knew not their intrigue
Nor had I, prescient criteria

Chillness of water benumbed me
Retrieved I, as cool as a cucumber to the bank

Is this terra God's palette?
Obviously! nature is the art of God.

Dark grey was lake's scenario
Stood reeds augustly amidst the lake.

Casuarina broke into tumult
When the west wind passed adriftting it

Glow worms scattered round the bushes
Heard I, croaking of frogs.

I felt languished by chillness
That pierced my chest and nostrils

Homeward bound, strolled I
For I had been there behind my father's back.

As being benumbed by drastic cold
I was at the end of my tether.

Soon felt I, in the arms of Morpheus
On the grass, supine anigh lake

By morning, I began to fly off at a tangents
When an highland lass harped on my shoulder

I began to know the ropes of that wintry night
For it cajoled me to sleep resembling lullaby

No human hardly be preponderate
Than a mother and nature.

Star Sweeper

Meg Horridge

"Hey, Madge, look at this."

I turn my head and see a red, flashing circle on Tara's monitor. Through training, kinetic launch, and the daily protocols of being in orbit, I've come to feel as though we're so prepared that nothing could possibly surprise us. But we're not omniscient; the monitors can only really show us what we expect to see.

"What is it?" I say.

Tara taps out a command to identify the object. Beyond the thick walls of the shuttle, a signal reaches out toward the UFO, bounces back, and becomes letters on the screen.

"Just as I thought," Tara says. "One of those old mega-constellation pieces of crap."

"Can I see?" I reach out a hand for the tablet. The Velcro holding it to the module rips sharply as Tara passes it to me. The data is still typing itself out at the bottom of the screen, listing log dates and propellant storage levels. It ends with a date and a sign-off. "It's twenty years old, shouldn't it be up for collection?"

"Nah, these old models still have five years on their lease. I remember when those things started launching—no regulation whatsoever. SU had to apply retirement dates in retrospect, and they were pretty lenient at first."

I scan the data again. "There isn't even a materials breakdown…"

"Wasn't required back then—like I said, no oversight. Don't worry about it, we'll get those figures when we need them. God knows we'll start picking up a lot of those soon enough." Tara takes back the tablet and glances through the data herself. "It'll be coming up beside us if you wanna take a look?"

I glide out of the flight deck and pull myself into the center module, bumping my hip on the entrance. I'm still not quite used to maneuvering about the shuttle, but it's hard to look clumsy in microgravity—no matter how badly I fumble, I still float.

At the cupola, I roll back the blankets on the windows, and the universe peers inside. It's brighter out there than you'd think. Every time I pull back these blinds, I find myself gazing out into the emptiness, jaw dropped, probably looking like my brain's fallen out my ear.

Tara says old shuttles didn't have viewing decks—there was barely enough space aboard for a few personal items, let alone a ring of giant windows. This one is big enough that I can lean the whole length of my body along the frame and gaze down at the Earth, 250 miles below. The Pacific is a vast blue carpet striped with clouds. I can't imagine staying sane here, in these cramped little rooms, without being able to stretch myself out on the ocean.

To my left, I spot the UFO—not unidentified anymore, I guess, but it was never flying either. It looks like it could, though: its solar panels are stretched out like wings. The solar cells are probably rotted to shit by now, burnt by overexposure. Its insides must be riddled with tin whiskers. On its casing, there is a large dent—from a collision with some other piece of orbiting debris—but I'd never have guessed how old it was if I didn't recognize the name printed in a block font on its side. A long-defunct company, whose engineers would have transferred their expertise and records to a Space Unification team at least ten years ago. The CEO is probably enjoying a lovely retirement somewhere while the courts are still trying to get an ecological genocide charge to stick.

It's not a satellite anymore; it's junk, designed to be discarded in one of the upper shelves of our sky to rot, drift, and eventually fall into the atmosphere. Burn up into pollutants. If not for Star Sweepers, it would one day slip out of orbit and hurtle back to ground. Best case: the remains would sink to the bottom of the sea. Worst: they'd crash through someone's ceiling.

"Nice view?" Tara's head pops up through the entrance to the module. Her greying hair, even tied back, bobs around her head like an air bubble. "We'll be coming up on Ladon in about 30 minutes—you'd better suit up."

#

I met Tara on the ground, three days before launch. Tall, stone-faced, early forties but already mostly grey. She approached me in the mess hall and stuck out a hand. The first thing she asked after I introduced myself was, "So how'd you get into this?"

I stammered at first. "W-well, I just stumbled into an internship by chance, really."

I was lying a bit—the truth would have sounded like such a cliché. I've loved space for as long as I can remember. My Grandma used to have a telescope in her garage, and when I visited, she'd set it up and help me find Venus. Looking back, I realize that space never looked right. It was never that clear, inky black like in textbooks—often, it was grey—and the stars never seemed bright enough, as if we were peering through tinted glass. Even Venus grew duller by the year.

It was only later that I'd learnt why—it turns out space debris is pretty opaque.

"What about you?" I said as Tara sat down across from me.

"Oh, I always knew I'd be an astronaut," she said. Her voice echoed through the hall amongst the rest of the chatter, where mine had cowered. "Build a colony on Mars or something—that's what the future looked like when I was a kid. Didn't imagine I'd end up an orbital cleaning lady, though."

"Do you like it?"

"It's all right. Still wish I was going further afield, but no dice."

"Probably a good thing. Can you imagine how much time and money it would take to get to Mars?"

She shook her head and laughed. "You'd make a great SU ambassador. You already know your lines."

I shrugged. "I want to make a difference."

"Yeah, you and everyone else in their twenties. Just don't expect to be changing the world on your first mission, OK?"

#

The metal braces grip my forearms, tight enough that I can feel them through my suit. I

squeeze the triggers under my fingers, and one of
the large metal hands layered on top of mine grabs
the outer rail of the satellite—Ladon 4, the one
we've come out here to retrieve. The exoskeleton
swings me smoothly up to her side, dragged into
slow motion by the vacuum. I am strangely numb to
the movement, as though the universe is shifting
around me, my body less of an agent than I'm used
to on the ground.

Behind me, two long grey cables trail from my
hip to the shuttle. With my metal hand, I unclip one
of them and attach it to the satellite's core. I
unspool the third, shorter cord that's clipped onto
my thigh and secure that to the unit too, closing the
loop between shuttle, satellite, and astronaut.

"Contact made," I say.

"How's it looking?" Tara's voice crackles
through the receiver in my helmet.

I cast my eyes over the satellite again. It's
smaller than the ancient one from earlier, its core
unit only a little taller and wider than I am. Its solar
wings seem to stretch out endlessly on either side.
"All good as far as I can tell. Nothing big missing."

"OK. Let's start with the panels."

Initiating the retirement protocol should be easy
enough—all I have to do is connect to the control
unit and type in the universal code. With little delay,
the solar panels begin to tilt and fold inwards,
towards me. They move slowly, eking out the last
dregs of the unit's battery power, reserved for this
express purpose. I imagine a whirring that, without
the benefit of an atmosphere, I don't hear.

The outermost panels come to a stop on either
side of me. I grasp the edges of the nearest solar
panel with my robot hands, tug it sharply, and it

comes free—like children's building blocks pulled apart. It's mostly metal and glass, and the size of my torso, but I don't feel the inertia of getting it moving; the exoskeleton applies enough force on my behalf.

"The chute is almost with you," Tara crackles.

I turn, hovering beside the satellite with the first panel in hand. A metal chute runs along the shuttle–satellite cable like a train on a track, only a few feet shy of me. Its gaping mouth creeps closer, unlit inside—a few feet in, it is darkness wall to wall. When it comes within a foot of me and stops, I ease the solar panel into it—a soft push, and the panel is off, sinking into the chute's dark innards, bound for the padded interior of the shuttle's cargo hold.

According to Tara, space shuttles never used to have cargo holds. I guess they didn't imagine they'd be bringing much back home with them.

I repeat the process for as many panels as I can reach and then prompt the unit to fold its wings in on themselves again to bring the rest closer. I keep working, trying to keep my mind off the sweat forming in globules on my skin, thick and unmoving.

"You're doing a great job, Madge," Tara says as I drop the last solar panel into the chute. "How you feeling?"

"You'd better buy me a drink when we get home," I huff. "This is harder work than I thought."

Tara's laugh distorts into a hiss through the comms. "The unit's next. You wanna take a minute?"

"No, let's get it finished."

"OK. Sending over the breakdown now."

On the small screen strapped to my forearm, a breakdown of the unit's material components appears line by line.

"Oof," I say, "86% aluminum."

"Yeah," Tara sighs. "It's a pretty small one, though."

I should know; I waited an extra six months for a mission that the team were happy to put me on. Ideal for a first timer—a simpler model, so less time out here in the suit. Less chance of me fucking up.

"I'm ready to get started when you are." Tara's worry seeps through the receiver, evading her attempts to hide it. "Do you want directions?"

"I'm good." The retirement protocol should do most of the work for me, and the unit's manual is ready on the screen at my forearm if I need it. "Opening the front panel now."

With metal fingers, I take apart the unit piece by piece, dropping each into the chute at my back: the hatch door, propellant tank, lithium-ion battery, and endless sheets of computer hardware strung together with multicolored wires. Technically, I don't have to be too careful with it—all the components will be catalogued and dissected back on the ground, the metals melted down and repurposed. But I don't toss the parts into the chute like they do in the training videos. Someone still made these, delicately pieced them together, and someone will have to pry them apart if I mangle them. These metal hands are magic, in a way: if they treat these parts like junk, they'll become just that.

Most of the way done, and I wish I could wipe the sweat from my brow. I bring my arm up, but it clunks against my visor, reminding me where I am,

the layers of glass and metal and nylon separating
my wrist from my forehead. I sigh. My small bunk
will feel like a king-size bed tonight, I'm sure.

Beep-beep. Beep-beep.

The beeping comes from just behind my left ear.
There's a red light flashing in my peripherals.

"Tara?"

Is it comms? This can happen sometimes,
temporary disturbance caused by dust or radiation.
The worst thing I can do is panic, but each silent
second that goes by quickens my heart rate.

"Tara, are you there?"

"I'm here. Madge, the suit is reporting higher
CO_2 levels than normal."

"Why?"

"I'm not sure. Keep calm and head back to the
shuttle, OK?"

"OK. Turning back now."

I reach down and unclip the tether connecting
me to the unit. My vision is a little spotty—I'm not
sure if that's from a meaningful lack of oxygen or
just adrenaline quietly entering my bloodstream.
The braces on my arms grip a little too tight, and
the pools of sweat in my suit are suddenly oceans. I
am not a metal frame with robot arms but a fleshy
human body. I am small.

I turn around and grab the cable that extends
back to the ship. The chute is already retracting, and
I go to pull myself in the same direction—
something pulls me back the other way.

I half turn, but the satellite unit gets there first.
The casing bumps into my side, sending a vibration
through every inch of my exoskeleton.

"What the—?"

The unit is still tethered to my thigh, following behind like a dog, never more than a foot away as I drift slowly toward the ship. I must have unclipped the wrong cable; the one that should be holding the satellite unit in place is following the chute as it retracts.

My hands are shaking. "Tara—Tara, I unclipped—"

"It's alright, just detach yourself from the unit and return to the ship."

"But we need to—"

"We can reattach later, Madge. Right now, I need you to focus on getting back inside."

The ship is surging towards me—no, I must be moving toward it, maintaining my momentum. I unclip the remaining cable from my thigh, but the unit keeps coming, following close at my heels. I don't think—I can't think, because the red light is still flashing and my helmet is beeping and this giant metal shell and the whole of the universe are crowding in on me from all sides.

I push the unit off my back with one metal arm. It spins as it careens away from me, from the ship, in the direction of the big blue ocean gleaming up at us.

My head stops spinning once the airlock is shut and the room is repressurized. Tara floats around me as she detaches the exoskeleton from my back and removes my helmet.

"Where's the unit? Did it go far?" I say, still gasping in air.

"Breathe, Madge."

"It was heading toward ground—if we don't grab it soon, it'll start re-entry."

"Don't worry about that right now."

"But we have to—"

"At the end of the day, we got the battery and the panels—"

"But it's almost 100% aluminum! It'll burn up and leave a hole in the ozone!"

Aluminum atoms tear into ozone molecules, stealing away half of the pairs, lingering unwanted in the air as aluminum oxide…

My throat is contracting. Each breath catches on my teeth.

"It's only a casing, Madge, it'll hardly leave a *hole*. You did what you could."

"No, I made a mistake, I fucked it up—I should've—"

Tara grabs me by the shoulders with both hands. With nothing holding either of us to the ground, we drift, and I have to put my arm out to stop my back from hitting the module wall.

"Madge," Tara says. "Stop spiraling and breathe. Your suit malfunctioned. You had to get back to the ship. Your life is worth more than a few ozone molecules, OK?"

I stuck in a breath. And another. First thing they drilled into us in training: don't panic. The worst thing you can do is panic. And here I am, on my first mission, panicking.

"OK," I say. "I'm sorry."

"I'll chalk it up to the low oxygen," Tara says and continues removing my suit.

#

```
2042.10.02 14:38:03
```
SU Star Sweeper D01
```
Report of unplanned re-entry.
Satellite Landon 4, casing and
antennae only. Approx. 2.7 m x
1.5 m, 60kg. Entering around
26°S latitude, Pacific Ocean.
2042.10.02 14:39:58
```
SU Observation Port 134
```
Report of unplanned re-entry
received. Identification
pending.
2042.10.02 14:46:35
```
SU Observation Port 134
```
Unplanned re-entry: object
located, (-25.981467,
-156.739274). Continuing to
monitor impact.
```

#

Tara and I started talking more after launch. There isn't much else to do up here. Between eating, sleeping and routine engineering checks, we only have each other for entertainment.

On our third day in orbit, we were sat in the center module together, eating 'lunch'—there's no time up here, but it was our second meal since waking, so we called it lunch. You need the illusion of Earth time to keep you sane.

After ten minutes spent chasing a floating M&M with her mouth, Tara piped up. "You know, when I first started out, I was on re-entry management."

"You worked for SU back then?" I said, eyes wide. "I'd just started secondary school when they launched that program."

"I get it, I'm old. Thanks."

"No, sorry, I mean... I remember when the first drones were launched."

They started burning up space junk two years into the Space Unification project. Unmanned missions rounded up old satellites and dropped them into the atmosphere over the ocean. Hunks of metal started washing up on shores, and bright streaks and bursts of colorful light would appear in the sky. SU's shooting stars, people called them—blue-green balls of light with orange streaks at their backs, turning to glitter. Space junk securing its final resting place scattered above our heads.

"I used to listen out for the alerts," I said, shaking my head. "It's so weird to think we were both watching."

"I'm not sure that's unique to us—a lot of people watched the re-entries. Didn't stop them sacking that program off after a couple years." I opened my mouth to respond but she held up a hand. "I know, I know—hole in the ozone, blah blah. Getting reassigned still sucked, OK?"

"Sorry." I plucked another M&M from the bag, let go, and it hung in the air in front of me. With a gentle tap, it drifted Tara's way.

#

I don't watch the video sent up from Observation Port 134. I stare out the cupola while Tara watches on her tablet. I hear laughter broken up by radio static.

"Completely destroyed upon re-entry," Tara says as the video ends and she puts the tablet on standby. "No harm done."

I stare at her. "No harm?"

"Madge, give it a rest, would you? Did you see how much you pulled off that thing, how much we're taking back with us? You did a brilliant job, especially for your first time."

"No, I didn't. I panicked and launched a hunk of metal into the atmosphere."

"You made a *mistake.* It happens. And a little unit like that won't have much effect in the long run. For heaven's sake, do you beat yourself up when you throw something in the wrong recycling bin?"

I think for a moment. "Sometimes."

"God, your generation!" Tara laughs. She pushes herself off the window and gestures for me to follow. "Come on. I wanna show you something."

When she begins playing with the ship's controls, I lean in to try and figure out what she's doing. "You're not taking me on a joyride, are you?"

"We're not going far. Just a slight adjustment…"

Outside in the vacuum, little nozzles spurt gas and nudge us this way and that. I stop watching—right now, it feels like we could be the next piece of metal plunging into the atmosphere.

After a few minutes, Tara shuts off the manoeuvre controls and brings up a camera image on the console. We're right above South America, a green expanse under a spotted blanket of cloud.

"What do you see?" Tara says.

"Er, I see… land?"

She tuts. "And on that land?"

"Grass? Bushes? Trees?"

"Trees! Exactly." She points to the upper left quadrant of the continent, which is almost entirely a rich, dark green. "When I first came up here, most of that land was yellow. This is the greenest I have ever seen the Amazon—the greenest it's been in almost a hundred years! Now, you tell me: is that good news or bad news?"

I hang my head; I know what she's doing. "Good news."

"Yeah—amazing news! And to add to that, we have a cargo full of materials—materials that *you* salvaged—that will mean no one has any excuse to go hunting for oil or ore there any time soon."

"OK, OK, I get the point." I can't help but smile.

The Earth has gone dark for the tenth time today, so we take the opportunity to watch yet another sunrise. Orange arms splay out across the blue curve of the Earth as the sun emerges from its brief slumber. Within a few minutes, it's over, the star becoming its usual ball of yellow light on a blue-black canvas.

I catch sight of Venus—the brightest star in the sky—and point it out to Tara, like I always do. It's bright, brighter up here than I've ever seen it through a telescope. And I could be imagining it, but it seems like every time I see it now, it grows brighter, brighter, brighter.

Working Around the Policy

Ben Nardolilli

Employment agencies are looking for an
experienced receptionist,
so I applied, bragging about being an expert of the
art of taking things in

In my email, I talked about riding out the shifts in
everyone's style,
the earthquakes in syntax, leaping from platform to
platform to be social

As well as dealing with a carousel of faces at the
top of the pyramid,
watching new power players on the rise, and the fall
of the end of history

There was always an adjustment to these and more,
lies coming
and going with latter-day revelations handled with a
perfect little shrug

I told them if current events that are now called
history were not enough,
and the switch from tape to bytes insufficient to
prove my abilities

They could open the attachment down below,
listing books I remember
processing and names of former lovers I cannot
manage to forget

Clepsydra

Ben Nardolilli

How long have things gone on and gone by?
Half a mug of water sits on my desk at the office,
It means morning is half lost, at least,
Pretty soon I'll be greeting with "good afternoon,"
And then "good evening" before leaving for the
train

But there's a full mug of water back home
On another desk, one rarely used for work or
pleasure,
What does that show? An evening has passed
But a morning has yet to come,
With sunlight to unwrap me from my bedsheets?

And in addition, there are the two coffee cups
Crumpled up in the nearby trash,
Each waxy one took me an hour to sip and finish,
But when? Were they the last first thing I drank,
Or did they go down with, or after my lunch break?

December Full Moon Special

Lost In The Void

Louis Faber

Wandering in the void
the bearded man
dragging a ragged tool belt
with a rusted hammer
says I built all this
and all you remember
with a bit of help from Dad.
It wasn't perfect
but you had to admire
my craftsmanship.
Take a short walking tour
of the Galilee
bits of my handiwork
are scattered about
just be careful
as you cross the waters
the stones just
below the surface
are a bit slippery of late.
I must say
I preferred working
in the valley
heaven knows
climbing that hill

was no party
particularly since dinner
set so badly.
It's no surprise
that my work
was so crude.
It's tough when
they give you
second rate materials.
In any event
I've got to go
I've got
a remodeling job
over at Jerry Garcia's.
He's not
very grateful recently.

Novelist on a Vacation

Damien Kelly

Sabotage. Espionage. Décolletage. Just a selection of the words that spring into my mind at random moments during the day. I like to think about them and how they sound – why do I like them, why do they appeal to me – it can happen over the space of a few days, or even weeks, and then they disappear to be replaced by something clsc. Ncbulous I might think to myself for no apparent reason… I'd be interested to know what that means. Another one for the commonplace book. A chugger blindsides me just off Crow Street as I'm meditating on the feel of the rough cobblestones underfoot and asks me to support some foreign or domestic cause or other – I actually didn't hear him. I politely decline, apologetically shaking my head: too many hills to die on, I'm afraid. Not knowing my deeply held opinions on all forms of injustice, be it dog fouling on footpaths right to the very, very top, he assertively and persistently reengages me with, what in my mind is, a clearly contrived friendliness. God does love a trier. I fix him with what I believe to be a death glare, seemingly to no avail. Read the room, I think. I've read Mackenzie m'lad – I understand insincere acts of compassion and the wish to satisfy one's own feelings all too well. I feel compelled to tell him that, sorry, I have far bigger issues: with my constant daily battles trying not to carry out acts of defenestration, strangulation, rustication, electrocution or self-immolation on myself as I look in the bathroom mirror each morning. In fact, I only stop short in telling him about my relief on a jazz-fueled date atop Casa Batlló when, nervously navigating the ornate draconic dreamscape of its soaring scaly rooftop terrace, I finally realised that I actually didn't want to engage in autokabalesis. He walked away with a tired expression, not quite sure if I was being serious or not… and that made two of us.

Continuing my walk, I come to a small cafe that I've been to a couple of times before and go in to have some eggy wegs for brunch. My server is without doubt the most beautiful woman I have ever seen, in person, I suppose. She looks like she could be a Kilkenny woman – or possibly even Tipperary – but I'd be reluctant to say for sure which; in fact, for all I know she could be from Dongeradeel. She has lustrous red hair with a hint of a kink, and these deep chocolate-brown eyes that I know always look like they're smiling. Dressed all in black, she… Now, how would someone of my capacity encapsulate this woman's ineffable allure yet remain somewhat tasteful. Could I actually do her beauty justice without mentioning her gloriously soft figure, her dimples of Venus. I can, almost, describe the feeling that such beauty affects in me, like a sudden kick in the guts, a rising pang, a *saudade* or *struggimento* – a *deseo ardiente* if you will. I refuse to look at her for the rest of my meal – she's just trying to do her job, I know – I don't need her to think I'm… looking. Do I really need to look at her for some kind of inspiration anyway? That's why I'm here after all: to travel, to observe, to have new experiences. My dear boy, why don't you just try writing? What are you afraid to write? Why are you afraid to write? Oh yes. The abandoned novella: *Tierra del Fuego*. An overlooked gold rush. Or so I thought. Sickened that a similar premise had already existed. And only 5.2 on IMDb. Blegh! I need to reset and step outside my comfort zone, maybe. She passes behind me in a rush and pardons herself with a soft hand on my shoulder – sorry, pet – as her quick, confident stride sends a flurry of amorous vanilla, lavender, cacao and ginger notes swirling invitingly in the warm August air. Titian's *Venus* may evoke something timeless, but I know I mustn't reduce this woman to a sensual muse. She's more than just a vessel for my hollow words.

Having finished, I take an Aircoach from Westmoreland Street to the airport, and towards my creative bolthole. 23,000 feet, 13,000 feet, 3,000 feet and the plane touches down in Schiphol. I board a double decker train to Amsterdam Centraal and cross a busy intersection to a train themed hotel facing the station, where I'm checked in by the gruff but ultimately friendly enough man at the front-desk. Peckish, I quickly throw my bag into my room and go looking for food, stopping at the first place I find around the corner: Global Kitchen. I eat quickly, ignoring what feels like a slightly cold patty, in my rush to get out and begin my work, to *flâner*, to disconnect myself and drift aimlessly to contemplate the city's unique, vibrant aura, to get a feel of its seedy underbelly, and fill a page or two in my journal. Oh no! Me innards start sloshing and squelching. Yes, I can definitely feel it. That was quick. My bubbling guts gurgle. Burnt Umber warning signs. A liquid foreboding. Raw Sienna. Oh! The runs is right. And run I must. Post haste. Where to? To the safety of my hotel. Sweating.

Clenching. For all I'm worth. Excuse me. Sorry now. Janey mack. Head gasket gone. Betrayed by a short order chef. Vincent Van Gocky. Forget lift. Take stairs. Oh, sweet Christ. Merciful Jaysus. Too close. Comfort. Ohhhh sweet porcelain saviour. *Inspectieplank*. Not necessary. Not today. Oof. So – how long will I be stuck in this damn-blasted hotel room, all on my own-io, left to my own devices; I wouldn't want to end up like that Dutch chap – Van Leeuwenhoek was it? – father of microbiology some say, largely self-taught, was holed up in a hotel room one time, ended up pulling the plum off of himself – idle hands and all that – then took a gander at the specimens he'd left round the place under his microscope, turns out, anyway, in the heel of the hunt that he only went and discovered spermatozoa. Came upon it by chance. Scuttering fuck.

After a few more visits to the old *badkamer* I decide to persevere with this trip. The writer that I keep hidden away from family, friends and colleagues is taking a break from stock replenishment to work on his secret craft. Retracing my earlier footsteps, I pass the infamous Global Kitchen again where my vengeful hopes of locking eyes with my unscrupulous poisoner are dashed. Bastard. I reckon I should probably try and eat something – oddly enough. Something bland but filling. Something to settle the stomach, maybe. I spot a crowded frites vendor and join the queue. One *puntzak* please. No sauce *Bedankt*. The guy just shrugs as he hands me my order. I walk onward through Dam Square and find a place to sit while I eat, when I notice a picture of Manneken Pis on the paper cone. This image penetrates the background of my memory, revealing to me something that I feel is an ominous premonition of my current situation and takes me back to a place next to a statue of a little pissing man. Warm and cozy in December, we seemed like the only two people in a crowded tavern. Strong Trappists and cured sausage consumed under the watchful eyes of dusty marionettes. Faded by repeated visits, these memories may lie but the truth remains. She softened me. I finish and walk on alone, criss-crossing the picturesque, canaled streets. No destination in mind, no fixed goal, just a hope that a path will reveal itself and span my great void. I come to an area where the streets appear to grow more crowded – ah yes – the notorious red lights. In and out of the streets I walk, passing by the red curtained window doors. *Kamer te Huur*. Mostly empty. Those occupied; however, the workers look at me like no woman has ever done before. Not one, but two, three, four are countenanced with this indescribable look in their eyes, a strange look, a wanton indifference. At first it seemed funny to me, maybe flattering and then… unusual? Is this how an ogled woman feels?

I stop for a drink at a hotel bar next to a canal that seems to be the main thoroughfare of foot traffic through *De Wallen*. The neon sign says Royal Taste. I order a glass of Texels from a barman who corrects my pronunciation with a single word, and I move next to a large open sash window with the intention of sitting and watching passersby. One of the chairs outside facing the canal frees up and I move to get a front row seat. I'm immediately struck by the unmistakable smell of either hash or weed or cannabis – I'm not quite sure – and what I assume is a cocaine dealer approaches and mutters something at me in a guttural language to which I instinctively wag my finger in the negative. It gradually dawns on me that I have almost every vice at my fingertips. I can remain the distant and watchful observer, hoping to dream up some compelling literary scenario or let the handbrake off and ideate in some altered state. The beer is not agreeing with me and is giving me a pain in me belly, so, acquiescing with the latter option, I Google a coffeeshop nearby. Google. Joyce didn't use Google. Or Wikipedia. Wikipedia. Kalipedia? Kalipedia... he certainly led me down a blind alley from beyond the grave with that one, the fucker. The queue is out the door at the weed place when I arrive – literally – I'm not one hanging around. So, I embark on another aimless stroll. A young kid – nine-ish – knocks on a window and waves at a lingerie-clad girl, who is busy texting on her phone, while the boy's parents look on laughing. In fact, I'm almost certain three nuns passed me a little further back, and not sexy nuns from a hen party or the Sexmuseum, actual nuns from an actual nunnery. Little old ladies in habits. A bizarre, artificial place, where innocence meets seediness.

This walk seems to clear my mind, and I begin to think that maybe consuming a space cake for the first time, on my own, is not such a great idea. I don't want to end up hallucinating that say: some eighteenth-century Dutch merchants with dreary, jowled faces under tricorn hats and curly white wigs and shapely fishnet stockinged legs critique my writing as – DERIVATIVE! – while scattering the pages of my unfinished, unwritten,

unstarted manuscripts into a canal and threatening
to stick tulips up my bottom if I can't prove that I
am literarily real in front of a throng of maniacally
laughing drunken tourists. Or failing that, fall into
one of these canals and get tangled up in a rusty old
High Nelly and become just another statistic. The
mighty, late summer's day ebbs towards evening as
my flowing mind leads me from *straat* to *straat*,
frustrated at the lack of inspiration encountered. No
golden seam unearthed. Stopping for a moment at a
picturesque bridge, my eyes follow the streaks of
light shimmering along the softly rippling water
towards the illuminated dome of the Basilica of
Saint Nicholas which stands before a backdrop of
blue and deepening indigo that fades into the black
of the coming night; and as a silhouette begins to
shroud the surrounding buildings, friends and
lover's legs dangle nonchalantly over the canal
bank, and point down towards the dusky mirror that
stirs my inner turbulence.

  There is a more night-time vibe now and I
feel I should go to a bar and relax, have a drink and,
most importantly, avail of their facilities. Passing
by several establishments I poke my nose inside –
too busy – and return to my rambling which is
beginning to feel all too samey. I find the sparsely
populated Cafe de Zon, which has an outside
terrace that faces onto a small, bicycled square, and
tip inside. I order a pint of Amstel and claim a high
stool close to the toilets. The glass is filthy – a petri
dish of possibilities. Here we go again. Can I risk
leaving it unattended? A slipped Mickey, perhaps?
Squirrelling the pint away in a secluded corner I roll
up my sleeves to undertake the dirty job at hand.
The toilets are an olfactory nightmare. The cubicle

hums with the stench of the day's piss. I can't in all good conscience sit down in here. I actually can't sit down – the seat is gone – broken off at its little hinges. And insult to injury, the bloody bog roll holder is empty; sodden cardboard tubes lie in pissy puddles on the floor. Another plan scuppered. I bottle it up and try to finish off my drink outside on the terrace when I get the sudden urge that it might be the time to move somewhere else – and so I do – swiftly through the maze of narrow and dirty streets, uncertain which of the common states of matter this urge actually is: solid, liquid, or gas. I can see the headline now: Arklow man arrested in Amsterdam on suspicion of defecating into *bosca bruscars*. The *Politie*, I dare say, wouldn't take kindly to a grubby-solo-sex-tourist type besmirching their beautiful city with his scoury shite, like a dirty auld sick calf.

It's officially nighttime in the now dark and brooding Nighttown and I wander past a smattering of windows lit by soft blue neon-bulbs, whose pastel glow emits a more alluring quality than the gaudy crimson. A captivating figure with a demure gaze waves at me, timidly. My pace slows as I gawk at her patent vulnerability. Then – I'm jolted from my trance by the unmistakable sound of an arse being slapped. I wheel around to the sight of a tall lady in just a phosphorescent lime green thong who opens her door and beckons me in with a curling index finger. Blushing, I decline with a smile – an urgent appointment – as she winks and giggles teasingly, feigning exasperation that the waving of her magic wand had failed to charm me. A gilded promise. The neon-redlit windows have started to fill up and more women try to grab my

attention. More people are engaging with them –
some serious, some in jest. I need to get away from
this part of town. It's not for me. I come to a
horseshoe enclave where I notice an Irish bar and
descend into its bowels to discover, much to my
delight: a clean and functioning toilet. With my
fears finally allayed, I attempt to drink a few pints
outside, straddling the verge of tipsiness next to an
annoying, overly affectionate couple who suck face
and coo at each other. Here I resolve under the
shadow of De Oude Kerk to change tack –
tomorrow I'll embrace the art and culture of the city
instead: *The Potato Eaters* and *The Merry Drinker*
– as I realise that the day's aimless wanderings took
me around a fruitless loop of, perhaps, a mere few
hundred yards.

Cold now but mostly rendered weary from
time spent in my own company, I decide to swing
back in what I assume is the direction of my hotel.
As I pass a number of sparsely occupied windows,
the incongruous nature of a monstrous church to my
right and a bevy of "fallen women" to my left is not
lost on me. Not ideal bedfellows. Hands in pockets,
feeling the dewy air counter my tiredness, I
approach a corner where I'll need to remember if I
turn left or right when a striking brunette beats
loudly on the glass with the palm of her hand and
invites me in. I smile and continue walking. She
opens the door and almost begs me to come speak
with her, please, just for two minutes. That look
again. I shake my head and turn right – the wrong
way – and glancing back I can see she is still
gesturing for me to come in, but this time a little
more irate. Maybe some inspiration does lie in there
– I think of those greats who found their muse in

secret chambers with seductive women. *Nu Couché*. My curiosity ponders the joy proposed.

I double back. Her curtains are drawn. He who hesitates. Flummoxed, I continue down the lane when out of the darkness another figure emerges and draws me irresistibly towards her room. A strange trembling seizes me, my eyes dazed, as my entire body seems to pulse in unison with my pounding heart. A price was agreed – Cristal from Dominica – though how that came up, I don't know. Or why it mattered? She's twirling slowly now and lifts her skirt to reveal soft curves. She moves closer to me as I pray to God that she doesn't kiss me on the mouth. Not wanting to offend her with my reaction. She sits me down on the edge of a bed and sheaths me with her luscious lips and then with steady breath this complete stranger begins an act of the utmost intimacy that to me feels – cold, robotic. I try to surrender myself to her but only an ill-fitting curtain keeps me from the indignity of being caught *in flagrante delicto*. My inner world ignites a paranoid fantasy of some transgression that will lead me to disgrace and punishment. Only by catching a glimpse of my brutish eyes in a mirror's reflection can I recover the poise to break the hex that came over me. Making my excuses, I leave under the immense weight of a humiliating sense of waste and shame. Again, I return to the streets and wander through the dark, sordid alleys and the scandalous gloom of the lanes – no glistering hope, no spark within – a feral soul drifting alone in the shadows.

The Glacier at Night

Samuel Goldsmith

We ran an afterschool art program, he and I.

We met at art school, when my life was dry as the bristles of my brush, the liquid in my paint-water cup clean enough to drink. I specialized in oil painting, he in ceramics. We calcined separately at first, but once we came to know one another, he fired and glazed me.

Visual artists exist only in schools. They vanish after they graduate, replaced by part-timers and mid-level office workers. The doubles resemble the original artists plus a couple of years and crow's feet. Artists hire them to condemn their bodies to the dangerous business of living.

Artists do not do their own stunts. They linger backstage alone, so solitary that none can say for sure whether there is such a thing.

But they are there. They are there.

After we graduated, he and I hired afterschool teachers to double for us at our art program. Yet, before long, the children spilled over the audience's rim and into something non-performative. They left the theater and they washed their hands at our sinks and they sat themselves at our coffee tables and they clasped our pillows close to their chests and the artists in us retired. The stunt work became the art, and the art became a memory.

Years passed.

One day, he had an announcement.

"We're going to do a language class now," he said.

To him, it was a matter of survival. Life or un-life. He never wanted to spin a wheel again.

It was Latin that he suddenly felt compelled to teach. But it was not truly sudden, the way nothing is. The way a volcano erupts in a flash and a rumble, with barely a warning, despite resulting from forces that had been predictably but invisibly building. I had the limited perspective of a Vesuvius observer, one who saw an ordinary mountain one moment and a plume of ash the next, a cloud that spelled apocalypse in a black alphabet I had yet to understand. Unseen in the hot kiln of the world, fissures of crazing chipped at our magma glaze.

"It's the foundation for so many other languages," he said.

"I won't have to choose between the Romance languages," he said.

"But it has to be languages," he said.

Neither of us understood the language.

"Help me study," he said.

I wondered about his vision for the art instruction. He said, "You're still thinking about that?"

I did not help him study Latin.

He taught it as well as a swim instructor who enjoyed floating down a river in a tube but lacked the courage to blow bubbles.

I rinsed the kids' brushes and cups alone. Insect carcasses accumulated along the edges of the kiln.

The miraculous oven was cold and unmovable. It looked like a glacier and sounded like a moonbeam.

"Ars longa, vita brevis," he said.

The parents understood the change in curriculum less than I did, but they also cared less. Of course they would have swooned over lumpy, blebbed vessels to place on their mantles, but they were just as happy for their children's noodles to hold the Latin root for "vessel" instead.

Years passed.

One day, he had an announcement.
"The kiddos need to move their bodies," he said.
"Have you seen what they eat these days?" he said.
"They need a bona fide physical education class," he said.
I saw only the two of us, alone.
"How about you teach it?" he said.
More crazing in our glaze.
"Perfectum est," he said.

I dipped my brush into the cup water, spun it like a skirt. The bracken tickled the bristles, licked the color off them, then flushed as if embarrassed from the intimacy of it. When a painter caresses a solid surface with a brush, it paints. When he caresses water with it, it unpaints.
I did not teach physical education.

"I can't do this alone ad infinitum," he said.

I wondered about his vision for the art instruction. He said, "You're still thinking about that?"

The non sequitur of painting and Latin lasted and lasted and lasted.
"You've had plenty of time to get used to this," he said.
He was not scolding me. I was not the child whose chin was flecked with crumbs of sweet chocolate contraband. No. I was the person looking into his dog's eye as he closed the door between them. He was whimpering, powerless.

This is all a metaphor. There was never any art class or Latin class. No paintbrush, no kiln. No crazing, no craziness. No monsters, no ocean. No years. No life.
He said, "If you make this into a meta-commentary, I don't think we'll be able to work together."
The kiln looked like a glacier and sounded like a moonbeam.

Metaphor — from *metapherein*: "(1) to transfer, carry over; (2) to change or alter; (3) to use a word in a strange sense."
meta ("over, across") + *pherein* ("to carry, to bear, to bear children")

I read a guide to field games instruction and understood it no better than I understood legalese. Nevertheless, I bought a set of cones.
I asked the students to paint them. The kids emblemed three with monsters from a world

apparently without rules of perspective. Three more were given remarkably generic sports images, all balls and limbs. Another received a fish-filled ocean decal. Others sported flowers and trees, houses and cars.

Yet, whenever I carried the stack of cones out to the field, the paint chipped away and was carried off in the wind, just dust, and they became nothing but plastic again. The monsters went back under the bed and the ocean dried up and the generic athletes trotted to the locker room and I turned around without setting up the game.

His artist had come out of retirement, I saw. I could not actually see the artist; like all artists, he was stored backstage and out of view. But he was there. He was there. The teacher I saw each day, sharing a location with me but otherwise sharing nothing anymore, was his double. It was the dramatis personae he had hired to endure living in daylight, waiting for darkness to fall so he could pass the baton to the artist. And here was I, flipping on the light switch whenever the double tried to dim them.

He was wrong. Ars brevis, vita longa.

Years passed.
I teach the afterschool art class alone now.

The day after our partnership ended, I heard a great groan from the direction of the kiln, as if the color from the sky had jolted awake. The glacier was calving. The existential sound echoed away,

and the sun went out with it. The only sound left in
my blinding night came from the moon.

Sagittarius Zodiac Highlight

Journeys of a Boundless Soul

Brooklynn Preston

Beneath the boundless sky I stride,
A seeker with a restless heart,
Chasing horizons far and wide,
A voyage born of eager start.

With fires burning deep within,
A spirit unconfined, untamed,
The world's a map, a game to win,
A canvas vast, unclaimed, unnamed.

I wander through the dawn's first light,
Embracing dawn's eternal gleam,
Pursuing truths beyond the sight,
A never-ending waking dream.

My footsteps echo through the trees,
A dance with wind and whispering leaves,
A quest for knowledge, moments seized,
In every breath, adventure weaves.

The open road becomes my muse,
A path where curiosity leads,
In every challenge, I infuse
A zest that sows both hopes and deeds.

I soar beyond the highest peak,
With eyes set on horizons new,
In every chase, I find my week,
A boundless sky, a limitless view.

My heart is wild, yet it's sincere,
A compass pointing toward the true,
Through doubts and fears, I persevere,
With courage fierce and spirit blue.

I cherish freedom's gentle call,
The chance to roam, to learn, to grow,
To stand beneath the sky's vast sprawl,
And let my inner fire glow.

No chains can hold my eager stride,
No borders limit what I seek,
For every moment, far and wide,
Is nature's voice that I must speak.

A soul that's born to chase the sun,
To find the meaning in the vast,
My journey's just begun—
A voyage ceaseless, free at last.

So here I walk through open gates,
A dreamer with a fearless heart,
In every step, I forge my fates,
A story born of endless start.

Titania in Autumn

A. K. Cotham

At the deepest end of our valley, there is a wishing well. And for as long as anyone can remember, instead of throwing in coins, people drip their blood. The stones bracing the outer wall are perfect for slicing. Blood makes wishes, stories say, because our bodies are water and what is life, after all, except one desire after another coursing through the rapids of our body until it is either satisfied or thwarted—and even then it can mutate into another white-water rush of yearning.

From the top of the valley, we watch pilgrimages to the wishing well, through nearly every season, the damp springs, clammy summers, and briskly mellow autumns; the winter road alone is silent. Down they go into the valley, these hopeful faces, and on their way back up, exhaustion is etched into their footprints. The hope has often been replaced by something else. It's not always easy to tell with what.

Nobody knows who built the wishing well or when—years ago, decades—or who built the nearby greenhouse that receives its sustenance. But there have been generations of caretakers for the deep end of the valley and for the well, the greenhouse, the altar inside the greenhouse, and for Titania herself—Titan Arum, *Amorphophallus titanum*, the corpse flower.

Titania blooms in the morning, thick with constant nourishment. When her spathe opens up its royal crimson interior and her pollen song is released, the pilgrims attend with their prayers—for health or wealth or fecundity or revenge or success, or something else they dare not speak of, waiting for a glimmer of something, anything, that rejuvenates their hope, keeps that white water of desire in a froth.

Stories about Titania and her suppliants are endless. Everyone knows someone who was blessed and someone who was turned away, and many who fell somewhere in between. We hear of visitors who entered the greenhouse and then ran, unable to bear it—scarred or frightened or angered by the powerful odor of rot, of bitter decay, of loss, whatever greeted them, for everyone is different. We call this group the *bled and fled* and true—we snicker. But, stories say, if you flee the greenhouse, your chance is lost forever. Titania remembers blood and disrespect. You are not welcome back.

If Titania chooses to sing your song, you listen.

***

Stories also say that Titania is at her strongest in the autumn, her last surge before winter hibernation.

So, when the summer wind changes and the valley trees begin to exhale their burnt golden breaths, my cousin Zoya and I, for the first time in our lives, join the steadfast line of callers along the road—all ages, all genders, all infirmities, all desires, none of us extraordinary, all of us unique.

The pilgrimage moves steadily down the valley. We see people we already knew and meet people that we now know. Everyone shares their own story, and often someone else's story. Some from far away have made it a true pilgrimage, traveling and camping for days, sleeping against trees or in each other's arms. Two sisters walk near us for hours, joyful and chatty about everything except why they're here. For some, the *do not speak your wish* superstition holds strong. But everyone impresses upon each other the same advice that has been passed down for generations: that *you must have patience* and *interpret wisely* and *not everyone gets an answer* and *you can't always get what you want.*

Zoya has one dogged wish and her hand remains protectively pressed on it, the new small swelling at her belly.

My wishes are somewhat humbler, given my prognosis. I simply want to live.

Hours pass. Footsteps plod. Food and drink is shared. Zoya, mildly sniffly with the changing leaves, carries a bundle of handkerchiefs. We reach the end of the valley in late afternoon. Zoya points out the wishing well—a distant structure toward which our line steadily weaves, in the middle of a green landscape dotted with vegetation, fences, sheep. Chatter grows quieter, more reverent, the closer we get.

And the closer we get, the more we smell the earth—loamy, deeply fertile, enriched with centuries of nutrients, as well as by centuries of decomposition and the breaking down of life not into dust and ash but into dirt, leaf, stem, root. *What breaks down always builds up again*, Zoya murmurs, tickling my nose with a vivid orange leaf.

Our well-trodden pathway goes first toward the well, and then beyond the well to bend and disappear under a dark green canopy of trees. A second pathway emerges from another point of the canopy, used by the visitors who have completed their mission. These people are too far away to speak to, but not far enough to ignore their expressions—quiet, beatific, weary, stunned, anguished. Some have clearly succumbed to being among the *bled and fled*. This close to those faces, nobody snickers.

Before we left, and as we walked, Zoya and I promised each other we would not be among them. That was the very least we could do for each other. We make that promise again as our feet step onto dirt, onto grass, into mud, and then as we reach the well.

Nobody pushes; people in line wait patiently for their turn. When two people leave the well, we slip into their spots. Several people are holding their reddened wrists or fingers over its mouth. The two sisters who walked with us stand quietly, pricking each fingertip with a needle. One man leans over and slashes his palm with a pen knife, shaking his hand into the depths. We had considered bringing a knife or needle, but the stories also say that using the well's stones itself gives strength. I graze my palm across a sharp edge. When the line on my hand merely appears red, I grit my teeth and do it again, slower and deeper, stinging, until there is a flow. Zoya finds a similar stone; it takes her only once.

We retake our place in line, others slipping into our spots at the well.

The sun is full and west. Murmurs travel up the spine of walkers that Titania is getting sleepy. What happens if the caretakers close the greenhouse before we get there? People worry. *We sleep against the trees*, others say. *We don't leave. We wait. Titania will be there.*

The bend into the canopy appears. Someone passes us going in the opposite direction, quietly counting—counting the number of people left for today, one of the sisters whispers. There's a commotion, a wail behind us, where the line gets cut off for the day. We breathe shakily in relief.

We round the bend and descend into a suddenly humid dimness. Ahead of us, by perhaps fewer than twenty people, is the deep viridescent glow of the greenhouse. As if by command, we fall quiet. There is no sound here except for birdsong and our shuffling feet. Even Zoya's sniffling has calmed.

The sisters in front of us go together into the greenhouse together, arm in arm.

I smell nothing but soil and forest and my cousin's sweat.

Finally, the caretakers motion us forward. Zoya and I inhale deeply, clasp hands, and step inside the greenhouse. My cousin lowers her handkerchief to her belly, determined not to flinch and show disrespect. I raise my chin. The door closes us in. Our holy minute has arrived.

And there she is, Titania, looming violet and husky ivory, seven feet tall of swaying majesty, glowing and serene under a strange greenhouse sunlight. The stink of organic decomposition, of old blood and fungus and pollen and other unknowable elements, is overwhelming, primal, and real. It enfolds us. Our eyes sting and water. Through our intertwined fingers, I feel Zoya's instinctive need to run. As well as my own—but I clench her hand as a reminder of her promise, and she does the same for me. We made it in time for Titania's autumn song. Neither of us will have the time to come back.

So we hold hands, determined to endure. Zoya's nails accidentally draw more blood from my hand. One fetid lungful after another, we breathe through the burn. My panic grows tighter. My cousin feverishly whispers her prayer-wish over and over, the one she has practiced for months now, watering red eyes fixed on Titania. I'd created no specific prayer, just an abstract appeal— *Please.* Surely Titania will understand what my *please* means. When she receives my blood and sees what is hiding. What else could I possibly be here for?

But now I wonder if it will be enough. As the stench grows deeper, breathable air growing thin, I wonder if any of this is enough. I can't be the first to have offered sickened blood to this formidable creature, but now I'm appalled at myself. How can Titania survive on what she is being fed? Why would she accept such poor tributes and grant such beneficence in return? What kind of covenant is that?

Shadows in the corner shift and the motion snaps my attention in half.

It's the caretakers at the exit door, moving toward us. Our time is up.

I realize, heartsick: This is not *bled and fled*. This is not terror, anger, or horror. This is, perhaps, worse—my last inadvertent thought is one of *doubt*.

That is acceptable to no covenant.

Swallowing, I look at Zoya, who doesn't yet notice the caretakers.

But because I am looking at her, I catch it: the moment that my cousin's fear, anxiety, the bleak weariness, all of it, falls away with the knowing, *the knowing*, that she will finally, after three losses, get her wish. She takes a deep, unhindered breath, exhaling with gasps of laughter, of relief, of joy—breathing a different air. Her eyes are still watering, but clear now. Her handhold is lighter, too, when she squeezes my hand.

I can't break my sweet cousin's spell, or her heart, so I squeeze back as though I agree—as though Titania had also sung to me, as though I hadn't alone ruined my one chance.

Zoya's joy will be enough for us both.

I accept the silence of the song that wasn't.

The caretakers are murmuring at our shoulders. Zoya lets go of my hand. Before we leave, though, Zoya pauses to put two fingertips to her lips, then to her belly, then into the richly striated, hickory-mahogany soil at Titania's base. Quietly, for my cousin's sake, I do the same, touching my lips and the soil and then—

—and then the lungful of decay simmers away, leaving me awash in something else, something altogether new and old and timeless—*a symphony of laughter, campfire smell, the flat-slap cold of lake water, wobbly bicycle chains and vertigo of swings, the purring warmth of pets under the night-blooming jasmine, the lemon verbena of our grandmothers, the cigars of our grandfathers, lavender and juniper and chalk and classrooms and asphalt and leather and sideways rain and scorching beach sand and stinky feet and icy snowballs and old bookstores and new cars and minty kissable breath and new babies and first loves and last loves*—memories loosen and swirl through me like a kaleidoscope, then are released into the pollen song, wisping into the air like a spiraling galaxy.

As soon as we understand each other, Titania gently releases my soil-stained fingers. I bring them to my lips.

And I too breathe freely, my eyes clear.

Zoya waits for me at the exit. Still basking in her own song, she can't see how my song, my wish, is now gathering around and showering her like fairy dust, like a soft sunbeam, and will only come alive through her once I am gone and her daughter is here. But she will.

Crosswalks: The Curse of Croesus

Robert Witmer

I was born in 1951, the year the world's first crosswalk was officially installed in Slough, England, where it was known as a zebra crossing. Questions of priority. Walk safely to the zoo my children, and snap your selfies with the eponymous quadruped that once grazed the wide savannah. Slough. To imprison. A state of moral degradation into which one may sink. Go safely children. Cast off that outer skin that is the perfect copy of the serpent from which it came. Beware the muddy ground, the hole filled with mire. A mass of dead tissue on the surface of a wound.

For the rest I am dumb, though if the streaking clouds could speak, such a tale of woe would we hear.

A suit insists the boys in lab coats cry wolf. A shot in the dark. A shell game. The music of chance. The opsonic index and vaccine therapy of pseudodiphtheric otitis.

Tyrian purple. The color of power. The smell of which hovered between rotting shellfish and garlic. The badge of noble youth. Opulence. Excess.

Wildfires. Floods. Thin air. Such stuff as dreams are made on. Pipe dreams. Oil. Unctuous and rich. Slick and sweet. Opulent. The physic of the field become an engine's lucifer. Light. More light.

Our *auto-da-fé*. The yellow press. The yellow peril. The sinful implications of a yellow book.

Yellowstone. To micturate in a caldera and spook a spunky bear. Beware. The danger. Do not piss off a ranger.

The boy on the hill. Rounded by sheep. Bored to sleep. There he lies they say. He would not toe the line. Sip your whine, Philistine, and pray. Bird of paradise. Bird of prey.

Know the plane truth. Attempts to fix the landing gear caused to fighter jet to think it was on the ground. At peace. Hot air. Follow your nose, the plane was told. A piece of goods. *Noli me tangere.*

He met Solon in the Peacock Saloon. *Just one for old times' sake.* So back and forth the bottle went, as they recited Shakespeare to a mirror on the wall.

> Methoughts I saw a thousand fearful wrecks;
> Ten thousand men that fishes gnaw'd upon;
> Wedges of gold, great anchors, heaps of pearl,
> Inestimable stones, unvalu'd jewels,
> All scatter'd in the bottom of the sea.
> Some lay in dead men's skulls, and in the holes
> Where eyes did once inhibit, there were crept –
> As 'twere in scorn of eyes – reflecting gems,
> That woo'd the slimy bottom of the deep,
> And mock'd the dead bones that lay scatter'd by.

Richard III, Act 1 Scene 4

The Old Man and the Sea

Robert Witmer

"We had our hands upon an idol of the clouds." –
Euripides

Riddled with lice, the local fishermen were gathering
violets when the blind poet appeared, stumbling along
the muddy road. *Have you milked your snails?* he asked
the frightened children, draped in purple robes. Viridian
waves shuddered over the bleached bones of shipwrecks
starred with asteroids, where when the sun goes down
the lonely conscience of the moon pulls back its wrack
of woe and the ooze of treasures drowned beneath the
thousand creases in the forehead of the melancholy sea
waits in vain to hear the mermaids singing to the lonely
hero's lonely queen staring through the pearly gates that
were her husband's eyes. *Do not box your reader's ear*
unless you have a salamander to show him, the rosy-
fingered poet whispered to the barnacle goose, alone
where it breeds a mushroom from the rotting timber in
the briny deep. But the sound he sought could not be
ascertained in the belly of the indomitable dark blue
waters, the unpathed wind-obeying brine. And so he
died, weary and old with measures still unfathomed,
treasured into something rich and strange, bard of the
tragedy of war, its brutal destruction, loss, and futile
suffering, home to an enduring truth of humankind, that
we harbor demons of dominance and greed and lustful
dreams of glory resistant to the better angels of our
nature.

The Wrath of Achilles

Robert Witmer

"Go to the ant and be strong."

Fingernails appear to grow on the dead, looking to some like life after death. It is, rather, the deliberate process of death, the wasting of the flesh around the nail plate. Kamikaze pilots cut their fingernails before their missions, sending the clipped nails to their mothers for remembrance, and the family tomb. I ponder these fingernail facts as I clip mine on a park bench, and watch an ant carry one away. The nail sways above the ant like a spar on Charon's boat. What the ants back home will do with my nail I know not. Perhaps it could serve as an arch to enlarge the anthill. Or perhaps these Myrmidons have their own Dr. Frankenstein, who would do one great thing: create a being to fortify the commonality, providing help in modifying habitats, tapping resources, and defending the colony against their enemies. A Prometheus of the emmets, a fallen angel desiring utopia in life beneath the soil. Harmony underground. Until the muffled drums of war sound and the plain is repopulated with warriors, locked in the mandibles of loyalty, fierce and bristling for battle. Everything now is more beautiful, for we are doomed. The sun sets behind the trees. That once underfoot is underground. Like us, ants bury their dead.

A Taxidermist and a Ventriloquist Lock Horns on Mt. Olympus

Robert Witmer

V: Look what you've done with your potter's wheel. You turned on the light and stuffed them after their kind.

T: And what do you do with the breath of life? Exhale from the mouth of a dummy.

V: You give to the dead a sense of being alive.

T: And you pretend to listen to a puppet playing the wise guy with your own garbled gab.

V: You fill them with a semblance of self that watches with unblinking silence from a dusty shelf.

T: The voice of your words, still, small, a pretense of being in a stillborn head. A simulacrum of existence with lolling eyes and disarticulated limbs.

V: And no sparrow chirped, no bird flew, no ox lowed. A craftsman of illusion you are.

T: The illusion of an independent self you maintain.

V: The appearance of life after death.

T: Body and soul music to spice up the performance.

V: Mere kindling for a pyre.

T: Whence the inspiration?

V: Wherefore the reason?

"Enough already," the assembled deities cried. "This misadventure we call man was nothing but a lame attempt to exorcise our boredom."

"Exercise, you mean," declared the Titan, son of Iapetus. "They never had a chance, born naked and bound to die, yet flattered by their mirrors with the image of we immortals, high on nectar, with ichor in our veins."

"Your homespun wisdom is folly. To pity fools and give them hope, and then to find they wanted more. They wanted to be gods."

"I take my cue from deeds, not words."

"Indeed. And so we shall translate your words into moans and groans. You think that you inhabit heights beyond the reach of grief. Misfortune wanders everywhere."

"Tyranny's disease."

"Things true, but sad. Necessity is all."

"What drove me mad."

"Another time."

And so it was that once again a meeting of the Higher Powers ended in disarray, with the loudest voices in the room holding sway.

Nothing Can Stop Me Now

Robert Witmer

He chased records like the Duke's hounds went after a fox. Five days on a pogo stick. Just to be named in a book named after a beer. The fastest yodel. The most jump-roping dogs. Eating a bicycle in fifteen days. The world's largest collection of cereal box records. The Monkees Greatest Hits. The Jackson 5. Rock and roll. From the unreasonable silence of the universe to the lived experience of the absurd. Death in chains.

Eventually he came to see that records were futile. Like Zeno's arrow he could never reach the end, always only halfway there, to be overtaken by something going nowhere.

He re-purposed his pogo stick to use for transportation. Pogoing from bar to bar. Dropping quarters in the jukeboxes and watching the mechanical arm slip the record from its resting place and onto the turntable. The rock of Sisyphus rolling forever away. A happy struggle for a higher fidelity. The blues uplifting tragedies. Come let me hold you, darlin'.

December New Moon Special

War Games

Sarah Das Gupta

Beneath the trees in a pool of green light
Gas-masked, they re-enact forgotten nightmares
long ago.
Children, voices muffled, sinister, search
the enemy in a phoney war.
Sitting on grass
beaded with stitchwort and blue bells
Masks abandoned,
Half-eaten sandwiches, lemonade bottles, torn
wrappers
lie littering
the wounded grass.

A green breeze gently wafts along the trenches
Beyond is mud
 Deep, bottomless
   Reaching beyond earth's bowels,
     World's end.
Drowned, the 'Glorious Dead'- skeletons, corpses,
single rat-ravaged arm.
Gas masks snatched from hooks on clammy trench
walls.
In lines, the Blind,
 clutching, groping, gasping,

stumble, unasked, uninvited, into Art and History.

In bright, summer sunlight,
they sit on the manicured lawn.
Old ration books clutched in small, chubby hands.
Girls in shining rainbow dresses,
anointed, sun-washed, blessed, unreal –
On a garden table, brown eggs nestle in baskets,
Plates of sugar slowly melt, brash bottles of orange
juice,
glowering cod liver oil.
The blonde shopkeeper eyes her wares
But now old ration books sanctify a magical
Midsummer feast.

On Finding a Dead Deer in My Backyard

Nolo Segundo

I saw them a few weeks ago. My wife called me,
something urgent--
so I left the computer and went to see what so
excited her.

Three deer, 3 young deer meandering around our ¼
acre backyard.
They look thin, she said-- I agreed
(not saying it was not a good sign with winter
coming near).

We enjoyed watching them through our plate glass
door, their
casual grace, that elegance of walk deer have when
unafraid.
They were special, even more than the occasional
cardinal
alighting in our yard like a breathing ruby with
wings-- so
we stayed as still as possible. I told her that deer can
only see
what moves, so we held ourselves tight like
insensate statues.

Two of these white-tailed beauties grazed daintily
on the ground
but the third was drawn to our giant holly tree,
resplendent

with its myriad red berries, like necklaces thrown
capricious.
I was concerned-- something alarming about even
deer drawn
like the proverbial moth-- safe, I wondered, for deer
or tree?

The triplets soon left our yard, as casually as they
had come,
and a week went by-- then one day a single deer
came back.
I say back because she went straight for the holly
tree, and
I banged on the plate glass door and yelled as fierce
as an
old man can yell to scare off the now unwanted
intruder, for
something told me the holly tree would be death to
the deer.

She fled, but the next day came back again, again
alone, and
again with eyes only for that tree, an Eve that could
not say
no to the forbidden fruit-- or berries or leaves it
appears.
Again I chased her away, and for a few days saw no
return.

Then one brisk morning our neighbor called-- he
saw what
we could not see in the deep green thickness of that
holly tree.
The doe lay sleeping under its canopy (so death
always seems

with animals, unlike a human corpse where
something is gone),
killed it seemed by berries or the leaves of the
innocent tree.

I called my township-- they said, put the carcass by
the street,
we'll send someone to pick it up-- but I couldn't, or
wouldn't.
Not just because I walk with a cane, and am old and
unsure
how such a moving would be done-- no, no, it was
more--
when I saw the deer lying sheltered beneath the tree
it loved,
the tree it died for, it seemed a sacred place,
consecrated--
and I could not bring myself to violate nature's holy
ground.

On Seeing an Old, Old Friend as One Plague Ebbs and Another Progresses

Nolo Segundo

He came to the restaurant
with his 36 year old daughter
who I said looked radiant
in her first-time pregnancy.

We were eating outside
that rare summer day that
smelled more of heaven
than earth and my wife
and I had got there first...

so I had prepared myself
for meeting my friend
of half a century after
almost two years and
two major operations
on his part (a triple
by-pass and prostate
cancer as he neared
the ninth decade--
I almost wondered
if he was showing off,
a Superman of old age).

Still, my heart creaked
a bit when I saw old Gus
and young Kate coming
to our table: he was smaller,
slower, less exact in stature
and speaking and I had to
strain to hear him even
though he sat close to me
but none of that mattered
for a miracle happened--
the subtle but resolute
miracle found in the
bones of liking, the bones
of friendship and the
unbreakable bones of love
as all those months since
two old men last hugged
had vanished as though
we had dreamt that lost
time and now we were
once again awake....

A Dead Love Poem

Nolo Segundo

I hold her negative image
between my fingertips.
I study the X-ray of a face
loved and hated many times--
the alabaster dots replacing
those brown eyes that tripped
the clown, my soul, one day…
when? but yesterday?

The teeth a blackish-gray, apropos
perhaps a corpse but not a dead love.
Hair blonder than Scandinavian sun
entices memory of cold-black beauty.
I hold like a hollow man the negative
to the light, to see through the breasts
I had fondled in joy as the long-running
melodrama returns to the stage but
I no longer sell the tickets, there will be
no audience, the show will flop, and
I will take up gardening for growth is
life and the perforated celluloid which
I hold so gingerly between fingertips is
dead, unalive, inanimate, its enlargement
suitable only for framing in my memory.

Postscript:
Where are the sounds now?
The slammed car doors, the yelling,
the 'bitch' calling, the 'bastard' calling,
all prompted out of rage and intimate fear
along with the looks, glances trimmed

by a smear of hate, faces badly packed in
anger, ugly...they lie buried now within
love's treasure chest, beneath the touching,
the emerald speckled kisses and eye-shared
secrets across peopled rooms....

The ugly is buried with the beautiful.

An Old Poet's Walk in an Old Graveyard

Nolo Segundo

He always liked to walk among the dead---
for him it was a secret pleasure to imagine
the lives of once breathing, thinking beings.
He would stop at each tombstone, curious
perhaps more than reverent, for he had long
known the body was just a set of clothes
the soul wears in a world where appearances
matter more it seems than what lay inside…

The old man liked to compare his years to
those chalked on each stone, continually
amazed that so many had died with fewer
years on their belts, so to speak—not
that he thought his 74 winters were a lot:
yet seen backwards in time, all the summers
and all the snows and all the fallings of dried
out leaves dying dressed in colors like kings,
all those memories wouldn't fill a large
basket in that living library called memory.

There was a newish looking gravestone with
one of those weather resistant photos of a
handsome young man who died in his 24th
year—the old man always wondered how
the young die-- by a rare illness, or suicide,
or was he doing something he should not
have been doing, and karma took notice?

In the years practicing his little lauded hobby
the old poet found old graveyards to be best,
for old graveyards have markers of lives that
turned to dust a long, long time ago: 100, 200
years for some-- but for the old poet it was as
though they had died yesterday, because they
were new to him, and his mind's eye could see
them all living life large again in their own slice
of time, in their own worlds, with beauty and
pain, with loss and joy, with grace and fear....

There were so many folks to visit: each one
whose little stone house he stopped by he
introduced himself to, said hello, wished
them well, and wondered about what sort
of life the woman who died at 36 had led,
or the really old man of 98 with the funny,
old fashioned name—did he regret missing
the century mark, the old poet wondered.

Some graves he did not like to see, for
they were the graves of babes, who
left the world less than a year after
they had entered it with such promise--
some died within weeks or months,
a few died the day they were born--
all spoke in stone of hearts broken,
of hope stolen, of love taken away....

Dinner At Eight

John Ganshaw

The table is set with champagne being chilled.
White napkins are ironed and formed into
bishop hats.
Cutlery polished and set, glassware placed
An intimate dinner for two awaits.

Candles lit as eight pm draws near,
The chandelier is dimmed, and my heart beats
faster with nerves. My lips anticipate the
touch of yours on mine.

Time goes by, and I still wait; the clock is
now approaching nine. Slung back in a
chair with another glass of bourbon in hand.
No call at all.

The Sun now rises, and morning calls. The ice has
all melted, and the candles have gone. I'm still
slouching, and the bourbon, too, has gone. The
dinner has burned, but at least the gas is off.
Still no word.

The dust has settled on all the dinnerware.
Cobwebs
strewn everywhere, Empty bottles on the floor, full
case was delivered at the door. I've been waiting for
the past five years, to feel the touch of love from
your lips.

All that lingers through these years, memories fade,
yet

you remain so clear. Cobwebs gather on the chairs; dust
gets deeper everywhere. I see you lying there, the day you
left me standing here.

Authors

KATHERINE EDGREN won 1st Place of the Poetry Writing Contest. She has two books of poetry: Keeping Out the Noise, (Kelsay Books) and The Grain Beneath the Gloss, (Finishing Line Press,) plus two chapbooks. Her work has appeared in Coe Review, Birmingham Poetry Review, Light, Hanging Loose Press, Orchards Poetry Journal, The Brussels Review, Third Wednesday, among others. She headed up a department at University Health Service, and served as a Project Manager through the University of Michigan, and as an Ann Arbor City Councilmember. She is a retired social worker and a grandmother of four.

Page 27; 115

ARNOLD JOHNSTON won 1st Place of the Fiction Writing Contest. His poetry, fiction, non-fiction, and translations have appeared widely in literary journals and anthologies. Arnie's recent books of poetry are In and Out: Love Poems (Kelsay Books, 2025), The Infernal Now (2022), and Where We're Going, Where We've Been (2020). His two novels are Swept Away (2021) and The Witching Voice, A Novel from the Life of Robert Burns (2009). His plays, and others written in collaboration with his wife Deborah Ann Percy, have won over 300 productions, readings, awards, and publications across the country and internationally. Arnie taught for many years at Western Michigan University, where he co-founded the creative writing program and founded the playwriting program.

Page 28

JESSICA KNUTH won 1st Place of the Nonfiction Writing Contest. She is the author of Animalia, a novel seeking publication. She holds an M.F.A. in Creative

Writing from Antioch University Los Angeles. Her writing has appeared in literary publications such as Pictura Journal, Phylum Press, Sky Island Journal, and The Manifest-Station, among others.

Page 8

ADEEB CHOWDHURY won 2nd Place of the Fiction Writing Contest. He is a writer from Bangladesh. His short stories and essays have appeared in Dulcet Literary Magazine, Black Fox Literature, Unearth, Brown History Magazine, North Star Literary, among others. Awards he has won for his writing include the James Augustus Wilson Writing Award, the Skopp Award on the Holocaust, the Feinberg Undergraduate Research Prize, and North Star's Best Nonfiction Award. He lives in Binghamton, New York, where he works in financial planning.

Page 60

JAY KVARNSTROM won 2nd Place of the Poetry Writing Contest. He is the Department Head of English at a charter school in Western Massachusetts. He lives in Granby, Connecticut, where he writes poetry that explores the psychological experience of landscape and the tension between social structures and personal history. He is currently working on his first manuscript.

Page 58

KENNETH BOYD won 3rd Place of the Poetry Writing Contest. He, winner and judge of the Royal Palm Literary Award (RPLA), is a neurodivergent poet and former jazz musician. His poetry appears in Wayfarer Magazine, Unlost, Flora Fiction, Of Poets & Poetry, Viewless Wings, The Ekphrastic Review, and elsewhere. His collection, Grasshopper Dreams, was released in 2023. Kenneth is a graduate of the UCLAx Creative Writing Program and an Assistant Editor of Poetry at

Southland Alibi Magazine. He enjoys life in the South with his wife and dog, Stella.
Page 69; 126

SONALI KOLHATKAR won 3rd Place of the Fiction Writing Contest. is an award-winning journalist, broadcaster, essayist, and author. She is also the founder, host, and executive producer of the long-running program, Rising Up With Sonali which airs as a radio show on 30+ radio stations around the U.S., as a TV show on Free Speech TV (DirecTV, Dish Network, Sling TV), and a podcast. Her nonfiction books include Bleeding Afghanistan: Washington, Warlords and the Propaganda of Silence (2006, Seven Stories), Rising Up: The Power of Narrative in Pursuing Racial Justice (City Lights, 2023) and Talking About Abolition: A Police-Free World is Possible (2025, Seven Stories). Sonali's debut novel, Queen of Aarohi, is forthcoming in 2027 by Red Hen Press.
Page 71

SHARISA AIDUKAITIS is a writer and college educator in upstate New York. Her poems have appeared in numerous print and online journals, including *Penstricken, Moss Piglet, The Quarter(ly), Drifting Sands Haibun, Sublimation,* and others.
Page 107; 109

JUNIOR BAKER.
Page 114

HEATHER BARTELT.
Page 106; 128

DAVID BLUMENFELD is a former philosophy professor and associate dean. Since 2022, he has been nominated twice for a Pushcart Prize. One of his pieces received a "notable essay" mention in The Best American Essays 2023, another was featured in The Best American Haiku 2023, and 10 of his works were finalists or received other high praise in literary magazines. Blumenfeld also writes children's stories and poems under the pseudonym, Dean Flowerfield.

JOE DEL CASTILLO.

CYNTHIA CLOSE, armed with an MFA from Boston University, plowed her way through several productive careers in the arts, including instructor drawing and painting, Dean of Admissions The Art Institute of Boston, founder of ARTWORKS Consulting, and president of Documentary Educational Resources - a film distribution company. She now claims to be a writer.

A. K. COTHAM lives in Northern California. One flash piece won first place in CommuterLit's Flash Fiction Week 2025 and another won third place in Brilliant Flash Fiction's 2022 writing contest. Other works have appeared in MicroLit Almanac, 50-Word Stories, and Microfiction Mondays, among other places.

WILLIAM DORESKI lives in Peterborough, New Hampshire. He has taught at several colleges and universities. His most recent book of poetry is *Cloud Mountain* (2024). He has published three critical studies, including *Robert Lowell's Shifting Colors*. His essays, poetry, fiction, and reviews have appeared in various journals.

ZAYN DORSEY.

LOUIS FABER is a poet and writer. His work has appeared among many magazines, and has been nominated and twice nominated for a Pushcart Prize and twice for a Best of the Web. His new book of poetry, *Free of the Shadow*, was recently published by Plain View Press.

DANEEN FOX has appeared in The Channel

Marker and has won The Poetry Society of Virginia's Student Contest. A classical musician, she writes with an ear for rhythm, striving to translate the things rather left unsaid into something hauntingly beautiful, crafting poetry that's both confession and reconstruction.
Page 143

JOHN GANSHAW began writing in 2023 and has published over 100 poems and essays, most recently in The Vault, The Well Street Journal, Men Matters, The Marbled Sigh, and Wayfarer. John writes in hopes that perhaps in some small way his words can bring truth, justice, and change to this fucked up world.
Page 222

JOHN GREY is an Australian poet, US resident, recently published in New World Writing, River And South and The Alembic. Latest books, "Bittersweet", "Subject Matters" and "Between Two Fires" are available through Amazon. Work upcoming in Rush, White Wall Review and Flights.
Page 129; 130

SARAH DAS GUPTA is a writer from Cambridge, UK who has also lived and worked in India and Tanzania. Her work has been published in magazines and anthologies in over twenty countries. She has won and been shortlisted in a number of writing contests including: 'The Fairy Tale Review'- fiction, 'The Bermuda Triangle Competition' – poetry, The Writer's College – Essay.
Page 211

SAMUEL GOLDSMITH is a writer, musician, and photographer who lives in Richmond, California. He writes so as to become a river, not a lake. Since beginning his publication journey in fall 2024, his work has appeared in *Gone Lawn*, *Gyroscope*, and others.
Page 189

MEG HORRIDGE is a UK-based writer of speculative fiction, currently working toward a PhD at Lancaster University that centres on writing a collection of utopian short stories. Their work has previously been published in Flash Literary Journal and The Cabinet of Heed.
Page 161

DAMIEN KELLY is currently living and working in his hometown of Carlow. He is also studying for a BA in English Literature and History with Dublin City University. His short stories have featured in the Autumn 2022 and Winter 2025 editions of *Empyrean Literary Magazine*.
Page 179

N. MOHANARANGAM.
Page 158

BEN NARDOLILLI is a scrivener and a theoretical MFA candidate at Long Island University. His work has appeared in Perigee Magazine, Door Is a Jar, The Delmarva Review, Red Fez, The Oklahoma Review, Quail Bell Magazine, and Slab.
Page 175; 176

LARRY PIKE's writing has appeared in a variety of literary journals and anthologies. His poetry collection Even in the Slums of Providence was published by Finishing Line Press. He lives with his wife, Carol, in Glasgow, Kentucky.
Page 145

BROOKLYNN PRESTON.
Page 195

NOLO SEGUNDO, in his 8th decade, became published in some 260 literary journals in 21 countries and 3 poetry collections published by Cyberwit.net: THE ENORMITY OF EXISTENCE; OF ETHER AND EARTH; and SOUL SONGS. These titles reflect awareness gained when he had an NDE whilst nearly drowning in 1971: of a consciousness

predating birth and
surviving death, what
poets since Plato have
called the soul.

KATE TELL.

ROBERT WITMER has
resided in Japan for the
past 46 years. His poems
have appeared in many
print and online journals.
He has also published two
collections of poetry,
Finding a Way (2016) and
Serendipity (2023). A
third book, Sunrise in a
Rabbit Hole, will be
published in 2025.

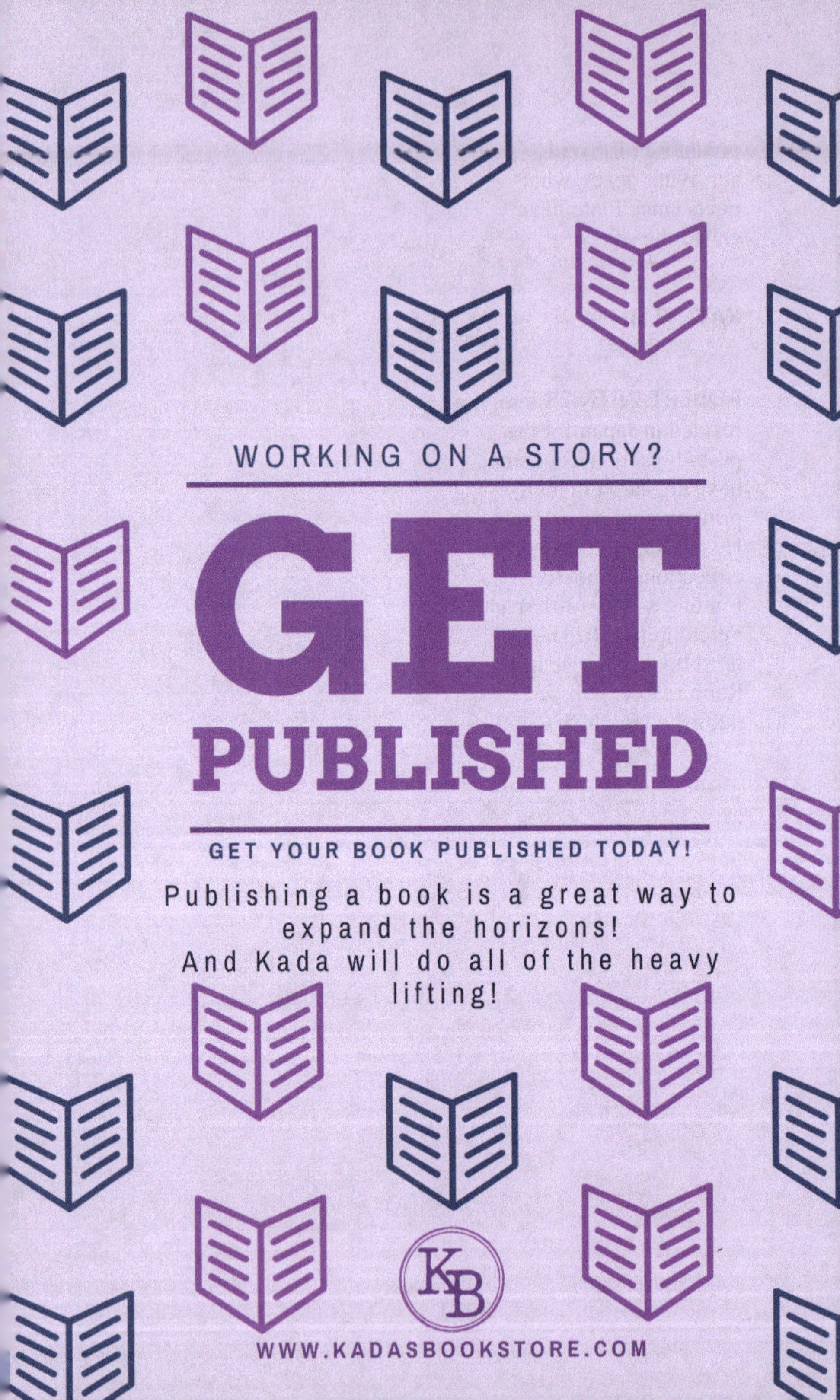

WORKING ON A STORY?

GET

PUBLISHED

GET YOUR BOOK PUBLISHED TODAY!

Publishing a book is a great way to expand the horizons!
And Kada will do all of the heavy lifting!

KB

WWW.KADASBOOKSTORE.COM

www.ingramcontent.com/pod-product-compliance
Lightning Source LLC
Chambersburg PA
CBHW061250210726
48293CB00003B/920